WHAT EVIL FORCE OF VILLAINY COULD STAND UP AGAINST THE SHINING HEROISM OF THE THREE AMIGOS?

The population of Santa Poco — men, women, children, chickens, goats, pigs, and flea-bitten dogs — was lined up to greet them. This was more like it! Waving and grinning, The Three Amigos paraded down the street, looking for a reaction from their fans.

But the villagers stared back gravely, some even grimly. Carmen and Rodrigo had been sent to bring back defenders, heroic men of such iron that El Guapo's *bandidos* would flee before them. Instead, the Sanchez children had returned with three gringo buffoons dressed in silver-embroidered clown suits. No wonder they were grim; who wouldn't be? When you need Superman, Mutt and Jeff just won't do.

"Whew," whispered Dusty sotto voce as he eyeballed the wary villagers, "looks like a tough crowd."

"They probably saw *Those Darn Amigos*," Ned speculated.

Lucky shrugged. "You're only as good as your last picture," he sighed. This gig was going to be tougher than they thought.

LUCKY .... STEVE MARTIN
DUSTY BOTTOMS .... CHEVY CHASE
NED NEDERLANDER .... MARTIN SHORT

THE THREE AMIGOS

THREE AMIGOS

A Novel
by
Leonore Fleischer

Based on the Screenplay by
Steve Martin, Lorne Michaels,
Randy Newman

PaperJacks LTD.

TORONTO   NEW YORK

AN ORIGINAL

PaperJacks

THREE AMIGOS

PaperJacks LTD.

330 STEELCASE RD. E., MARKHAM, ONT. L3R 2M1
210 FIFTH AVE., NEW YORK, N.Y. 10010

PaperJacks edition published January, 1987

ISBN 0-7701-0566-1

THREE AMIGOS

Chapter One

Mounted men. At least two dozen, perhaps more. Rifles pointing up like a line of deadly pickets across the sun-drenched Mexican horizon. The horses feel their way on nervous hooves up the rocky slopes surrounding the old mission. The men do not speak; their faces are grim under the shadowy brims of their dusty sombreros. They ride slowly now, conscious of the loose stones under the horses. Later they will ride faster. Much faster.

The dusty, bleached-out plaza of the humble little Mexican farming village of Santo Poco is dozing quietly under the blazing basin of the late afternoon sky. The men have been away since sunup, laboring in the cornfields or grinding the freshly husked grain at the mill wheel. The women who have families are busy in their dirt-floored kitchens, getting the evening meal ready. Those women who are widowed or who have never married are busy at foot-powered sewing machines, stitching serapes that bring the village a little extra money. They will continue to work at the Singers' until evening brings darkness. There's no sense in lighting the lamps at this time of year; although the days are growing shorter, daylight still lingers and lamp oil costs money.

Nothing is sleepier than a Mexican village in the year 1916. Even the dogs don't bother to scratch their fleas. Why should they? A flea has to live, too. *Como no?*

It's a profound canine philosophy born out of a stray's observation that the seasons progress in a natural and inevitable procession from planting to harvest, from spring to winter — a country philosophy that says, "Live and let live; there will probably be enough for all. If not, then maybe next year." Besides, Santo Poco dogs have so many fleas that it hardly pays to scratch.

Another peaceful day is drawing to its end. Farmers are stacking the cut cornstalks into sheaves which will be carried from the fields by wagons drawn by yoked pairs of patient oxen. It is the beginning of the harvest, and the men have worked hard today, their machetes rising and falling in an uninterrupted rhythm which suggests a bountiful crop.

The corn has grown tall and full in the ear, the silky tassels bright yellow, the kernels bursting with sweet juice. *Gracias a Dios*, it will be a fine harvest. The last ox carts, heavy with corn, are creaking slowly toward the village. A couple of barefoot *muchachos* wielding braided corn-stalk switches run alongside the wagons, hitting at the beasts, urging them to go faster, without noticeable results. The oxen merely swish their heavy tails to drive away the buzzing flies and continue at their usual plodding pace.

Down at the river, the beautiful young girls — Rita, Pepita, Lolita, Conchita, Rosita, Estrellita, and Juanita — are washing clothes, scrubbing them with handfuls of pumice and slapping them on the clean river stones to loosen the soil. As they do the village laundry, they laugh and chatter and toss back their glossy black hair, conscious that they are young and pretty, and still standing poised on the brink of life.

The town appears deserted. Only the younger children are still playing in the cool wet dirt around the tiny fountain in the plaza. The older girls are busy helping their mothers with the household duties; the older boys are working side by side with their fathers in the fields. A few fat chickens, a pig or two, a family of goats, and children under nine years of age — these, plus the inevitable stray and philosophical flea-bitten dogs — have the central square of Santo Poco entirely to themselves.

Nobody is at the water pump near the cantina; hours ago the women had drawn water into their large clay *ollas*, gossiped for a few minutes, and returned to their other tasks. A few *mujeras viejas* are squatting on straw mats near the granary, using crude mortars and pestles made of porous lava rock to turn dried corn into *masa*, tortilla flour. The grinding of the mule-powered granary millstone as it turns endless circles is the only sound breaking the stillness; that, and the clucking of the chickens as they peck at the dry earth for tasty worms and *cucarachas*, an occasional bark from a hungry dog, and the squabbling of the smaller children playing knucklebones.

Strung out in single file along the ridge, silhouetted against the copper sky, the men ride faster, urging their horses onward, cruelly raking the sweat-soaked flanks with their razor-edged spurs.

In mid-September the days grow noticeably shorter. The farmers rise earlier, at 4:30 a.m. instead of five. But this morning *Mamacita* Sanchez got up at four to get the cooking fire going, light the oil lamps, and pound corn flour into tortillas. She had not yet formed her long black hair which was just beginning to be touched with gray, into its customary braids. A bitter beverage vaguely resembling coffee heavy with chicory was bubbling away in a battered graniteware pot held on an iron rack over the fireplace. Refried beans for the breakfast tortillas were heaped on a colorful pottery plate, and two or three fiery green chilies — they give a man stamina as well as heartburn — were dished out and waiting.

At daybreak, Papa Sanchez, as usual, came in from the outhouse, rubbing the sleep from his eyes, already dressed in his work clothes. His drowsy brown fingers fumbled with the drawstring holding up his simple white cotton pants. He wore a much-patched white shirt over his trousers and his feet were bare except for *h]uraches* which had seen better *dias*. When Papa Sanchez put on his straw hat with the cracked brim, he was fully dressed. Now he and Rodrigo would eat, while *Mamacita* packed a takeout lunch of tortillas with refried beans and chilies, wrapped in corn husks to keep them fresh.

After breakfast, Papa Sanchez and his fourteen-year-old son Rodrigo would walk a mile and a half to the fields to tend their crops. This would take twelve hours, maybe thirteen, not counting the lunch break. Then, weary and fulfilled, they would trudge back to the village for a welcome evening meal of tortillas with refried beans and chilies.

This agrarian scene was reenacted daily during the growing season, not only in the Sanchez *casa*, but in every little shack, shanty, adobe *casa*, and hut in the village of Santo Poco. *Como no?* What more could the good life have to offer? Surely Santo Poco was the center of the known universe. These sturdy peasants might not be rich, but they made a living.

Now that harvesting was beginning, they all had to start working hard for a change — sixteen hours a day instead of the usual twelve or thirteen. This, too, would be fulfilling. Soon there would be fresh corn in plenty for the delicious tortillas. Soon they would make fiesta.

The riders are getting closer, breathing more quickly, a dark excitement rising in their chests under the bandoliers of rifle bullets. They are throwing laughing remarks to one another, evil and lewd remarks, accompanied by gross gestures. Soon. It will be soon.

Down at the riverbank, Conchita, Lolita, Rita, Juanita, Estrellita, Pepita, and Rosita are gathering up the clean clothing; washday is over. They have been gossiping and laughing as they worked, teasing one another about boy-friends and potential husbands. But the distant sound makes them look up in sudden fear, their laughter abruptly silenced. Are those hoofbeats? Mounted men with rifles? Oh, no! Laundry forgotten, they run swiftly on bare feet, slender brown legs flashing under full skirts, to give the alarm.

In the cornfields, terrified peasants throw down their machetes and run as fast as they can to the safety of the village. Even the usually placid oxen roll their eyes in fear. They, too, hear the horses. They, too, know what evil is about to befall Santo Poco. Better get back to the corral on the *doble.*

Except for a few ambitious (or backward) peasants still rummaging in the fields, the workday is nearly over. It is dinnertime; the sun hangs low and orange in the Mexican sky. In every small *casa*, whose walls of adobe mud are adorned with creeping bougainvillea and trumpet vines, under roofs of red clay tile, families gather around rude wooden tables, eagerly reaching for more refried beans.

In the Sanchez home it is no different. Mother Sanchez and Carmen, her beautiful gypsy-eyed eighteen-year-old daughter, serve the men with gladness in their hearts and tortilla flour on their aprons. *Casa Sanchez* is a house befitting the elder and unofficial leader of the village. Larger than most, it is comprised of three whole rooms. Two bedrooms are very small, only six feet by seven, and Rodrigo has to sleep in the kitchen with the burro, but three rooms are nonetheless three rooms. On the wall of every room hangs a crucifix on which is nailed a carved and painted image of the Holy Jesus, looking distinctly

Mexican. His tormented eyes, His anguished mouth, the pain and suffering on His thorn-crowned brow are a source of endless happiness to the Sanchez family.

As always, Papa Sanchez calls down a blessing on their simple meal. The old man, his face scrubbed and his hair neatly combed, sits in his customary rush-seated chair at the head of the table; to his right his son Rodrigo and, across from the boy, his sister Carmen sits demurely, eyes closed in prayer. Under the high collar of her modest dress her slender figure is concealed, yet its gentle curves are hinted at; such beauty is difficult to hide. A thick tangle of hair, a soft black cumulus cloud — or is it cirrus? — brushes her tender shoulders and neck, but it is bound up behind in a ribbon. If the ribbon were loosened, Carmen's hair would cascade down her back almost to her slim waist.

As always, Mother Sanchez — *Mamacita* — is the last to sit, waiting first to see that everyone else is served. When the blessing ends, they raise their eyes to Jesus, cross themselves, and dig in, grabbing up the tortillas, crunching the peppery chilies, and belching discreetly.

Outside the *casa*, the sun is setting over Santo Poco. Soon it will drop behind the foothills of the Sierra Nevada to the north, and night will fall. The last slanting rays turn the adobe walls of the little homes to reddish gold, and filter through the leaves of the gum trees surrounding the tiny fountain with its tiles of blue and yellow that stands in the middle of the town square. The granary is quiet. It has shut down for the day; its heavy seasonal work has not yet begun. When the corn has been harvested, the granary will swing into golden hours, but now the large grinding wheels and nearby storehouse, which holds the food supply for the entire village, are silent. The church is quiet; it's open for business only on Sundays. A few cooing pigeons flurry around their nests in the bell tower. The cantina is quiet. In the little corral on the edge of the village a handful of plump cattle — the most evident sign of wealth in the prosperous village — are sleepily turning a last few mouthfuls of dried grass into cud as a bedtime snack. In peaceful silence the world will soon be ready to grab some z's.

Um, hold the phone. Are those hoofbeats in the distance? Nah, impossible. Nobody ever visits Santo Poco. Nobody except . . . uh-oh. Shit.

The riders come up over the ridge that looks down upon the sleepy little village. For a minute or two they sit there, every man loading his rifle. Their horses are lathered with sweat, but the riders sit easily in the saddle, eager for their work — and for our story to begin.

Papa Sanchez looked up, his face filled with tortilla and refried beans, an unbitten chili pepper in his hand. He cocked his head to one side, listening. Fear filled his eyes, and he barked out an order in Spanish, which fortunately everybody understood. The entire family sprang into a frenzy of activity.

Rodrigo instantly went for the burro, dragging it out of the kitchen with one hand wrapped around its tail, while the other cradled the family pig closely to his chest. With the animals braying and squealing in protest, he shoved them into an earthen cellar disguised to look like a rubbish heap and locked them safely inside. *Mamacita* and the lovely Carmen scrambled to hide the platters and bowls of food, while Papa Sanchez grabbed the blankets and any other movables he could lay his hands on and stowed them away out of sight.

The hoofbeats had now become unmistakable. Riding men, two dozen or more. Armed men. Dangerous men.

Outside, in the streets around the plaza, the peaceful dozing had given way to wide-awake panic. The women of Santo Poco were scurrying hither and yon, snatching up chickens and children indiscriminately and hustling them indoors. Even the flea-bitten dogs and the randy cats were shooed inside, under cover. One villager had thrown open the corral gate and was moving out the village's collection of fat cattle, herding them into the cantina, out of sight.

The hoofbeats grew louder as they came nearer. Louder and more terrifying.

From the fields, the overtime workers came scrambling pellmell for home. Even the pair of slow, placid oxen yoked to the corn cart had picked up speed, almost trotting, as their huge brown eyes rolled wildly in their sockets. The little boys with the switches had by now disappeared into the safety of their adobe houses, but switches were no longer necessary. Those oxen were *moving*!

From the direction of the mountains to the north, a cloud of dust appeared, ominous, pregnant with meaning. Riders, many of them, coming this way fast. Moving hell-for-leather toward the sleepy little Mexican village of Santo Poco. That could mean only one thing. One rotten, dirty, lousy, scuzzy thing.

All through the village, shutters were pulled tightly across windows, and bolts banged hard against doors. Beds, dressers, and other heavy furniture was piled up against locked doors for additional protection. The stench of fear spread throughout Santo Poco as the riders got closer to the town.

The streets of Santo Poco stand silent and empty, the houses locked and barred. Even the insects have taken cover, frightened away by the ever-louder pounding of the hooves, a pounding that shakes the dusty earth and makes the *cucarachas* nauseous.

Into the empty town they ride, rifles held high, lathered with sticky sweat, their lips flecked with foam, their eyes rolling in their heads. That's not a bad description of the horses, either.

Bandidos. Evil *bandoleros* who prey upon the weak and the working, extracting from their labor-filled days the meager rewards that keep the poor little suckers alive. Cutthroats who laugh at misery — ha! ha! — and who snatch milk from babies and steal the last crust of tortilla from the poor. We're talking serious rotten *bandidos* here.

The armed riders assembled in the square and reined in. There were a good two dozen bandits, plus their leader. But where *was* their leader? Oh, here he comes now. Here comes El Guapo on his coal-black stallion.

El Guapo, the most feared of the feared, the most despised of the despicable. El Guapo, upon whose head had been placed a price no man dared venture to collect. While the gringo authorities were busy chasing the notorious Pancho Villa around the Mexican countryside, the even more notorious El Guapo was left free to rampage, terrorize, loot, rob, maim, kill, burn, rape, and generally make a nuisance of himself.

The boss bandit rode into the center of the plaza and pulled hard on the reins. Whinnying fiercely, the stallion Maricón reared on his hind legs, forefeet pawing the air. When Maricón's feet touched earth, his hooves struck sparks, and the bandits broke into a grim-sounding cheer. How they loved their leader!

He sat erect in the saddle, his evil, bearded lips chewing a loathsome cigarillo. El Guapo was ugly — grossly, awesomely ugly.

He was well-dressed though. El Guapo's clothing was travel-stained with desert dust and mesa mud, but under the stains was a jacket of fine wool and a serape woven in a colorful striped pattern. He wore a pair of leather chaps around which a gunbelt was buckled, holding two monster revolvers with pearl-handled grips. Over the serape, twin bandoliers crossed his chest, each of the ammunition belts bristling with cartridges for the fine Springfield rifle El Guapo brandished. In the saddlebag that hung from Maricón's back was a machete; that was for close work.

He wore a rough bandanna around his head to absorb the sweat. Over that, pushed back off his brow and fastened with a leather lanyard under his chin, was a huge sombrero. Once it had been a pleasant shade of gray, but after many years of wear and tear, plus the sweat from the leader's brow, the color had changed to something indescribable and not appetizing. El Guapo was sentimental about that darned old hat, and no amount of persuasion could get him to trade it in for a new one.

He had a small-boned dark-skinned face. His eyes were small and set deep into his head; his hair was grizzled and cut short, and he wore a short grizzled beard to match. When he smiled evilly, which he did often, being that kind of guy, the sun flashed off the gold teeth of which he was so justly proud. That kind of restorative dentistry doesn't come cheap.

All in all, he was an impressive figure, unless you were standing downwind of him. His importance was enhanced by the price on his head — ten thousand pesos, alive or (preferably) dead.

As befitted their lower station, the other *bandoleros* weren't dressed as well, but they, too, came completely equipped with sombrero, sérape, Springfield rifle, and smell.

El Guapo wheeled his horse around and took a quick narrow-eyed survey of Santo Poco. Except for a handful of stray and homeless mutts, the town was locked up tighter than a virgin's fiddledeedee. He scowled, then gestured abruptly in the direction of the granary.

At once several of his men dismounted and broke down the granary doors, coming out with sacks of milled corn, which they loaded onto the saddles of their horses.

Raising his rifle to his shoulder, El Guapo squinted down the barrel to the sight, took aim, and fired one shot at the bell in the church tower. It struck home; the bell reverberated loudly, scattering the mutts and sending them scurrying off with their tails low.

As the clanging died away, the bandit chieftain raised his voice.

"*Buenas tardes, señores y señoras.* How nice of you to welcome me once again to Santo Poco. Jefe!"

At once his second in command kneed his horse forward.

"*Sí,* El Guapo?" Jefe was a skinny little rat of a man, and a dirty, stinking, bootlicking toady, too.

"Jefe, maybe they do not know we are here."

Jefe took up the jest with eagerness. "El Guapo, that cannot be. We made so much noise. Maybe they are hiding in their houses."

El Guapo's little button eyes widened in pretended surprise, and he placed one hairy brown hand on his serape over his left bandolier, roughly where his heart would be — if he owned one. "Hiding from El Guapo? But why? They must know I mean them no harm. Jefe, bring them to me."

Grinning wickedly, the toady reached into his saddlebags and brought out three sticks of dynamite wired together. Jefe handed the explosives to El Guapo, who lit the fuse from the glowing end of his cigarillo and handed it back. Jefe spurred his horse forward to the nearest *casa* and tossed the lethal bundle onto the brick doorstep. At once the door opened and the family ran out, just in time to see their home blown to smithereens.

The villagers of Santo Poco needed no further convincing. One such demonstration was more than enough. Doors opened all over town, and men, women, children, goats, dogs, and pigs gathered in frightened huddles in the middle of the plaza. They brought their chickens with them, piling them up for El Guapo's men. The Sanchez family was among the crowd.

As he saw the hapless farmers cowering with fear before him, El Guapo smiled his awful, evil smile.

"My friends, it is good to see you again." He looked coldly down into Papa Sanchez's face.

"Old man, you remember me?"

"Yes, El Guapo."

The gold teeth flashed ominously. "You have so little to offer me," the bandit leader continued. His voice was as oily as his hair as he indicated the few sacks of corn and the squawking chickens tied on the pommels of the saddles. "This will not do. You know how much I have always depended upon your generosity. Winter in the mountains can be . . ." Here the bandit broke off as his little black eyes took in Carmen's delicate beauty. His gaze lingered on a tiny gold cross that hung around her neck, then moved down to her breasts. El Guapo licked his lips.

". . . long and hard," he continued. "Even the clothes I wear were made by the women of your village. They are beautiful, are they not?"

He preened a little, stroking his serape, but the cold, hard smile never left his face.

Sanchez drew in a deep breath to keep himself from trembling. "El Guapo, last year's harvest was very poor. We have had barely enough for ourselves. It has been — "

"He lies, El Guapo!" interrupted Jefe, the dirty little rat. "Let me kill him!"

But the bandit raised one calming finger, and his second in command fell back. "Jefe, Jefe, we are not animals," El Guapo said softly. "We do not kill people for no reason."

Pouting, the second in command kicked petulantly at the dusty earth. "Sometimes we do," he muttered to himself.

Once again Sanchez wondered, as he wondered every year about this time, why so foul-looking a bandit chief was called by the name "The Handsome One," while the rabbity second in command carried the title of "Chief." It was a complete mystery to him, but go figure *pistoleros*.

"Continue, old man," said El Guapo in that same too-soft, overly polite voice that sent chills racing down Sanchez's backbone. Tugging at Maricón's rein, he urged the stallion closer to the village elder. His eyes never left the slim, virginal body of the beauteous Carmen, who glared icily back. The bandit leered at her, wiggling his eyebrows, but his overtures fell on stony ground. No way was Carmen interested. She was saving herself for Señor Right.

"This year the harvest will be good. And when it is in, we will be happy to share with you what we can spare," pleaded Sanchez.

The greasy smile left the bandit's face, replaced by a scowl like a thundercloud. "What you can spare?" he hissed. "*What you can SPARE?!*"

A powerful hand shot out like a striking cobra, seizing Sanchez by his patched shirt and lifting him clear off the ground, *huraches* dangling. Now villager and bandit were eyeball to eyeball.

"Can you spare the lives of your women?" grated El Guapo through his clenched gold teeth. "Of your children? What can you spare, old man? When the moon is full, we will return! Fatten your cattle and gather your crops, and pray that the harvest is a good one! *Vamanos, muchachos!* Let's go, fellas!"

The stallion reared, and the bandit hurled Sanchez roughly into the dust. The old man's wiry body fell among the cruel hooves of the departing horses. Dimly he heard his wife and daughter screaming as the bandits' horses rode roughshod over him, kicking him from side to side on their way out of town, making an example of the old man to strengthen El Guapo's threats. Goddamn, they were a mean bunch of horses!

The sound of the hooves retreated into the distance, in the direction of the mountains. The bandits were gone, at least for a while. There was a reprieve, but only until the moon was full, which would take place, according to the best astronomical calculations and the natural folk wisdom of the farmer, probably next Thursday.

Sanchez lay choking in the dust, blood mingling with the dirt on his ragged clothing. His family rushed forward and helped him to his feet. Standing groggily, he groaned in pain, but there were no bones broken, *gracias a Dios*. Assisted on one side by his wife and on the other by his son and daughter, the old man limped to his *casa*, where he collapsed with a groan into his chair.

Tears of embarrassment stung his eyelids, and he brusquely waved away the glass of water offered by Carmen. He was supposed to be village elder, looked up to and respected. Sure, he'd tried to stand up to El Guapo, but what the hell use was it? All he'd gotten out of it was a collection of lumps and bruises and the imprint of a hoof on his you-know-what.

Rodrigo could not bear to witness his father's humiliation. His eyes brimmed with burning tears as he rushed back out into the street.

The villagers had mostly dispersed by now, slinking back into their little adobe houses with the busted doors. Only a handful remained, chewing over the topic of the day, the threatened return of El Guapo and his bandits.

"The next time he will leave us with nothing," said Carlos bitterly.

"At least he will leave us our lives," pointed out Pedro, an idiot who always looked on the bright side.

"*Sí*," retorted the other sarcastically. "So that we can plant another crop for him next spring."

This the boy could not stand to hear. "*Cobardes!* Cowards! Did you not see? They almost killed my father! Why did you not stand beside him?" demanded Rodrigo hotly. "You have guns. Why did you not use them?"

Carlos shrugged a little uncomfortably. "Yes, we have guns, Rodrigo. And we can use them," he conceded. "But not like El Guapo and his men." He shook his head sadly, already defeated.

"Then we must find men who can teach us to fight!" cried Rodrigo passionately.

"Rodrigo, you are very young," replied Pedro with peasant patience. "You do not understand. Our life has always been this way, and it always will be. We are farmers."

Carmen appeared in the doorway, her lustrous dark eyes flashing with militant fire, her high collar heaving with emotion. "Rodrigo is right!" she declared huskily. "We must find men who can protect us!"

"And what would we pay these men with?" demanded Carlos. "Santo Poco has no money."

For the space of a heartbeat, Carmen's face clouded with doubt. Then fire came back into her eyes and she raised her chin stubbornly. "We will find a way. We have no choice."

Rodrigo looked questioningly at his sister, but she merely tightened her arm about him. Her lovely face was grim, her luscious lips set in determination. When she looked like that, there was no arguing with her, and Rodrigo felt better already. If there *was* a way, Carmen would find it. After all, just as she'd said, it wasn't as if they had any other choice.

Chapter Two

A Mexican border town attracts the dregs of both societies — a limbo neither quite *norteamericano* nor *mexicano*, yet the worst of both. Oh, there might be a handful of negligible differences. Instead of serving rotgut whiskey, the shabby bars serve rotgut tequila. The whores are dyed brunettes instead of dyed blondes, and you pay in pesos, not dollars. But the essentials are the same. If you have something illegal to sell, like rifles or rum, or something illegal to buy, like arson or murder, then mosey along to a town like Diablo, and you'll make your connection lickety-split. Only thing is, if you sleep there overnight you'd better not close your eyes.

But to Carmen and Rodrigo Sanchez, Diablo looked like Paris, France. Dressed in their Sunday best, riding down the main and only street on their little burro, the two couldn't help gawking and rubbernecking at all the wonders. In their wildest dreams, they had never imagined so exciting a metropolis, so vast a center of sophistication and culture. Why, Diablo boasted a livery stable just for horses and mules so the folks there didn't have to sleep with them in their kitchens. There was a boarding house that served home-cooked meals of refried beans and tortillas and the ever-popular chili peppers for the outrageous sum of fifteen cents; there was even something called a telegraph office and other buildings they couldn't even begin to guess the uses of. Many of the crumbling walls of the village bore defaced and faded portraits of Venustiano Carranza, Mexico's legally elected *presidente*, with dirty words scratched in, misspelled, over the man's features.

By contrast, the "Wanted Dead or Alive" posters of the notorious Pancho Villa were as fresh and unsullied as the day they'd been pasted up, and were regarded with pride by the residents of Diablo. *These* were art, and Villa was their hero. To the Sanchez kids, who had never been out of Santo Poco in their lives, Diablo appeared like the capital city of the world.

As the burro made his slow and cautious way down the main drag, an ancient Reo turned the corner, chugging and clanking, black smoke pouring from its decrepit tailpipe. At the sight and sound of the automobile, the *burrito* froze in its tracks and its eyes grew round with wonder. So did Carmen's and Rodrigo's. None of the trio had ever seen a car before. *Santa Maria*, this was one up-to-date city!

Most of the activity in the town appeared to be centered about the tavern, Cantina del Borrachos, a sleazy honkytonk that seemed to Carmen and Rodrigo very impressive. The hitching post in front of the bar was full; it wasn't easy finding a parking spot for the burro, and they watched a steady stream of ugly men with pock-marked, unshaven faces slouching into the cantina. This had to be the "in" place favored by desperadoes.

"We will find the men we need in there," said Rodrigo a bit uncertainly, and Carmen nodded her agreement.

Tying up the burro, the brother and sister entered the cantina with some trepidation.

The bar was noisy, echoing with the loud cursing and angry threats of really nasty people, but the minute the two Sanchez kids walked in the door, all sound ceased and every dirty head, every stubbly face, every bloodshot eye turned to glare at them.

Here was a grisly and motley collection of gunslingers and badmen, of shoplifters, cattle rustlers, barn burners, pickpockets, check kiters, smugglers, bandits, highwaymen, burnouts, border raiders, cutthroats, assassins, child molesters, scuzzbuckets, and party animals. Taken together, the sight of them was scary enough to cause Rodrigo to take one nervous step backward and look for the door.

But Carmen was not so easily intimidated; she was determined to mask her fear. Their mission was too important. She squared her shoulders, making her round breasts wobble under her simple peasant blouse. Ignoring the single harsh intake of breath among the men, she spoke up in a clear voice that trembled a little at first, then rose clearly over the noise of the cantina.

"Señores, we are from the village of Santo Poco, and we have come here to ask for your help. A very great injustice is being done to the people of our village. A man named El Guapo is threatening the very life of our village. We are looking for men who are brave enough to stand up to this tyrant. We are a poor people, but we can pay you —"

At these words, a rustle of interest and approval swept the bar.

"But not with gold or silver —" continued Carmen.

Another rustle, this one of disappointment and disgust, as the desperadoes turned back to their drinks.

"With something far greater than either —"

The men turned back again expectantly.

"The honor of fighting and perhaps dying for a cause that is just!"

As she spoke those inspiring words, Carmen tossed her head proudly and the gold cross around her neck moved and twinkled in the dim light of the cantina, mesmerizing the men.

From one corner of the bar, one awesomely ugly man rose from his chair and approached Carmen, grinning like a shark. He carried a rifle, and he looked as though he could use it.

"Señorita, a moment. . . . Perhaps I can be of some assistance." He was a long-legged gringo and a fugitive wanted in every state from Texas to Missouri. "Ah'll help you, darlin', but first you must help me. . . ." With one strong arm, he drew the girl toward him roughly while the other bar rowdies laughed.

Carmen reacted instinctively, slapping and clawing, but he was too strong for her. She felt an overwhelming repulsion as his twisted mouth, with its rotten teeth and foul breath, pressed itself to her red lips, stealing the kiss.

Moving swiftly, Rodrigo dodged in for a well-placed kick, and, cursing, the ugly man was forced to let Carmen go. The two Sanchez kids turned and ran, not stopping for breath until they were at least a block from the cantina. They were sick with disappointment and disillusion.

"They are no better than El Guapo," spoke up Rodrigo bitterly as they straightened their clothing. They will not help us. No one will help us."

But Carmen's face had taken on a strange expression. Her head turned to the sound of organ music coming from a nearby building. Where there was organ music, there must be an organ. And where there was an organ, God must be present, for what else but a church has one? She seized her brother's hand tightly.

"Rodrigo, you must have faith. The Holy Mother will help us. Come." She drew him toward the sound of the music which came from a large church at the far end of the town plaza.

Diablo must not be such a bad place after all. So many

people were going into the church that it was quite crowded when Carmen and Rodrigo managed to squeeze inside. The little church in Santo Poco was never as crowded with worshippers as this. Almost every seat in every pew was already taken. The Sanchez children dipped reverent fingers into the little font of holy water by the threshold, crossed themselves, and went in.

But what was this? Where was the altar? Where were the painted statues decked in gold leaf? Where was the Lord Jesus with the real blood trickling from the thorns around his brow and cascading from the Five Blessed Wounds? Everything appeared to be hidden behind a screen of some kind. And the lights were out; no candles had been lit and the church was dark, except for a strange beam of light coming from a hand-operated film projector. Everybody's eyes were fixed upon the blank screen, suspiciously like a bed sheet, that was supported by a flimsy tripod. The pipe organ was being played slowly by a queer-looking man in a lavender necktie, but for the first time Carmen realized that the music was not religious.

She looked at her brother, bewildered. "This is not a church! Where are we?"

But Rodrigo did not bother to reply, because, suddenly, with the whirring of the aged projector, a photograph was flashed upon the screen. Miracle of miracles, the photograph actually began to *move* at a rapid though flickering speed!

First, the title appeared on the screen. *Los Tres Amigos*. The Three Amigos. Carmen's eyes grew round with wonder at this most marvelous, unheard-of thing. Three men rode into the Mexican countryside and came closer, so close that one could almost touch them, larger than life. Rodrigo gasped and shrank back, then relaxed, grinning. This was the best thing he'd ever seen in all his fourteen years on earth.

Madre de Dios, how handsome these gringos were, so dashing in their odd costumes!

They represented Hollywood's idea of how Spanish grandees and wealthy landowners dressed. Carmen had never seen or even pictured a grandee, so she didn't know if the costumes were right or wrong. She only knew they were so beautiful her heart leapt in her chest. It was thrilling just to look at them.

The three men were wearing tight black pants with wide, belled-out legs, ruffled shirts, and broad cummerbund sashes bound around their waists. Their jackets, short in the Spanish-Mexican style, were encrusted with what must surely be real silver or gold embroidery. The lapels were embroidered, the sleeves were embroidered, even the trouser legs were decorated down the sides with bullion threadwork. Their six-shooters were holstered by thick leather belts with silver conchos. On their boots they wore gleaming spurs of an astounding size, big enough to stun a horse with one kick.

Around their necks were tied kerchiefs, larger, silkier, and cleaner than any kerchief the Sanchez kids had ever seen, and on their heads were the biggest sombreros in the world . . . no, in the universe. They were larger than umbrellas, and they were heavy with embroidery that matched the rest of the costumes. Carmen sighed with longing. They were more beautiful than women, these three, and far better turned out. The girl wasn't sure whether she was sighing for the gringos or their outfits.

Even their three brave steeds were fashion plates. The horses' saddles, made of hand-tooled Spanish leather studded all around with silver, were higher and grander than any ever encountered in the real West; they must have weighed a good sixty pounds apiece. The horses' bridles were also silver-mounted, and, if the film hadn't been silent, the bridles would have been heard to jingle quite merrily.

All three men were heavily armed with large-caliber nickel-plated pistols that lit up the screen with the glint of dangerous metal, while tied on to the pommel of the

saddle of one of them was a huge lariat, shiny with new-
ness. The three were absolutely dazzling in their
magnificence.

"We are The Three Amigos!"

The title cards were in Spanish and English; the film,
of course, was silent. In 1916, the art of the motion picture
was only twenty years old, still under the drinking age
in most of the 48 states. Yet it had already come a long
way; it had created a new race of people — movie stars.

The organ music became uptempo and Carmen's
breathing became faster and shallower as each hero in
turn rode in for his close-up. Never had she seen strong,
exciting male faces like these!

"*Cabalgamos!*" We ride! Ned Nederlander's face grimaced in defiance of evil. Smaller than the other two
heroes, he wore an expression of impish confidence under
his broad sombrero.

"*Luchamos!*" We fight! This was Dusty Bottoms, who,
with white teeth clenched a cocky grin, looked as though
he could fight or laugh his way out of anything.

"*Amamos!*" We love! And now Lucky Day's face, with
its Roman, almost imperious profile under *yanqui* blond
hair, came looming onto the small screen, filling it with
a strength of purpose, yet, at the same time, with the
promise of *amor*.

Carmen didn't doubt it for an instant. But at this moment the drama began to unfold, and, caught up in the
excitement of it, she forgot everything around her, forgot
that she was in a crowded church pew filled with ripe-
smelling, unwashed border-town bobtails. All she could
do was keep her astonished eyes glued on the action on
the magical screen, and on The Three Amigos. This was
so real! This was life itself! This was Carmen Sanchez's
first moving picture.

"But in the village there is trouble," warned the title
card, and suddenly there they were, in the heart of a
little Mexican village. Carmen gasped. It was Santo Poco!

The same adobe houses clustered around the same little town square with the same dusty fountain and the same bell tower on the church. The same farmers in the same patched cotton clothes and rope-soled *huraches*, the same seamed and work-worn faces. But, no, how could that be? It was not Santo Poco itself, but a village nearly identical to it.

And now, flashed on the screen was a band of hideously ugly raiders, very like El Guapo and his *bandidos*, tormenting the villagers, taunting the women and striking the men. The prettiest of the village girls was struggling desperately in the brutish arms of a *bandolero*. Carmen heard Rodrigo cry out in terror, and his boyish hand stole into hers for reassurance.

"Only one thing can save us now! The Three Amigos!" said the title card in Spanish and English, and here came a close-up of the beautiful girl's face, not so different from Carmen's own, but now suddenly alight with hope.

Next came a tracking shot of a cloud of silent dust and the Amigos came riding toward the village on expensive horses while the organ music galloped into a suitable equestrian theme. The lustful *bandido* looked up toward the horizon, and a look of craven fear crossed his swarthy face.

"Oh, no!" proclaimed the title card. "It is The Three Amigos!"

And now they came riding into the village, their faces glowing with courage, their large six-shooter guns blazing. The bandit leader, a grotesquely made up actor with unnatural eyebrows and a Fu Manchu mustache, defied them like the scummy villain he was.

"You will die like dogs, Amigos!"

But Dusty Bottoms merely smiled boldly in answer. "No, we will not die like dogs. We will fight like lions!"

Truer words had never been printed on a title card. Fight like lions they did, each Amigo in his own spectacular way. For they were here, there, and everywhere, all at the same time, each with the strength and the courage of a dozen riders, defying the overwhelming odds against them, scattering the badmen like chaff beneath their horses' hooves while the photogenic grins never left their faces. How easy they made it appear!

Dusty Bottoms had drawn a knife from its scabbard and, with a lightning throw, had pinned one unfortunate *bandido* to the door of the cantina, where he struggled to free himself.

In one instant, Lucky, the one with the Roman profile, had his lariat coiled in his hand, and in the next instant it went whistling silently through the air, lassoing four fleeing bandits at once and bringing them down like helpless steers. Lucky hoisted the rope and tied it to a tree limb while the audience gasped, and the four bandits, their leader among them, dangled high above the ground, their legs kicking vainly as they shook their fists and screamed curses.

Meanwhile, little Ned Nederlander, his hands filled with lead-pumping pistols, was performing astonishing tricks of horsemanship and gunmanship simultaneously. For each bullet shot from his six-shooters, at least three bandits seemed to fall.

What an Amigo! What a man!

As the church audience yelled approval, the remaining bandits, the fortunate ones who were still alive, scrambled for their mounts and got their asses out of there. *Como no?* What evil force of villainy could stand up against the shining heroism of The Three Amigos?

While the wicked desperadoes fled, defeated, over the horizon, the village elder and his beautiful dark-eyed daughter, the one who'd had the near-miss with the would-be rapist, gratefully approached the Amigos.

"Here is the hundred thousand pesos we promised you," read the title card as the old man offered up a sack heavy with gold, and the young girl offered up her heart.

Ned Nederlander reached down from his saddle and

took the sack, hefting it with appreciation. He looked at his buddies. The Three Amigos exchanged glances and grins, then Ned gallantly tossed the bag of gold back to the villager.

"Our reward is that justice has been done!" flashed on the screen.

Leaning down, Lucky Day kissed the pretty girl, whose face yearned with admiration and . . . desire. Then, for the last time, a close-up as he turned his noble profile to the camera for a moment or two, or three. . . . or five. . . . What a profile! What an Amigo! What a guy!

"Let us give the Amigo salute!"

Then The Three Amigos sat tall in their saddles as they executed their world-famous trademark Amigo salute. Hands crossed on chests — one, two. Then on their hips — three. Their horses reared, their mighty hooves striking the sky. Now see them riding off into the sunset — gallant, proud, defiant, bold, heroic, dashing, gringo, handsome, you-name-it-they-had-it — with the cheers of the grateful villagers and the tears of the grateful maiden still sounding in their ears.

"Fin," read the title card. The End.

The lights came on, and the people began filing out of the church.

But Carmen and Rodrigo remained behind, enraptured, still staring at the blank screen as though they expected The Three Amigos to return at any moment in the flesh. Never in their lives could they have imagined such heroism. These three were the very men that Santo Poco needed — men who defied danger, who laughed in the teeth of overwhelming odds, men who could ride and rope and shoot and kill bandits without losing their smiles or mussing up their hair.

"Rodrigo," breathed Carmen, "I did not know such men existed!"

The boy nodded his agreement. "With three men such as these, El Guapo would not dare to enter our village."

His sister stood up, determination lighting her lovely face and shining from her lustrous eyes. This was what they had hoped and prayed for, what they had journeyed to the big city to find.

"We must let them know we need them," she declared. Si, but how? As they left the church, Rodrigo was shaking his head negatively.

There was a panel truck parked at the curb. Carmen saw the three-sheet four-color advertising poster pasted on its side, emblazoned with the names and the images of The Three Amigos. She approached to inspect it more closely. On the bottom line of the poster, just above the copyright date, an address: "Goldsmith Productions, Hollywood, California." Just as Carmen had predicted, the Holy Mother had sent them help.

It was a decision of a moment to send them a telegram. At first Rodrigo held out for getting back on the old burro and heading straight for Hollywood, because he'd always wanted to cross the border, but Carmen's decision was unshakable. A telegram would bring help more quickly than they could bring themselves. The corn was ripening fast in the fields, the harvest only a few days away. El Guapo would be back soon, and these men were needed at once. There wasn't an instant to spare.

The two had never been inside a telegraph office, with its mysteriously modern machine clicking in code. Rodrigo eyed it doubtfully as Carmen dictated the address to the telegrapher, who wrote it down slowly with a blunt pencil stub. He was a large middle-aged man in sleeve protectors, wire-rimmed bifocals, and a green celluloid eyeshade.

"Are you sure this machine will deliver the message?" The boy's furrowed brow displayed his suspicions.

"It must, Rodrigo. It is the only way. . . . The Three Amigos, Goldsmith Productions, Hollywood, California. Have you got that?"

"Ha . . . meee . . . gos," wrote the telegrapher, nodding, and waited for Carmen's message.

"I still say we should go there," put in Rodrigo stubbornly.

"No, Rodrigo, there is no time." Carmen turned all her attention on the crucial contents of the telegram. "We have seen your deeds and think you are very great. We can pay you one hundred thousand pesos —"

"A hundred thousand pesos!" the boy interrupted with a horrified gasp. "Carmen, we do not have one hundred thousand pesos! There is not that much money in all of Mexico!"

But the girl tossed her head impatiently, and her dark hair tumbled fetchingly about her face. "Don't worry, Rodrigo. They will refuse it. Haven't we just seen them refuse to take money? They are interested only in justice. But it would be an insult not to offer it to them."

She was right, of course. The Three Amigos were not interested in gold, only in seeing justice prevail and good triumph over evil. Rodrigo had seen it with his own eyes, but it was only courtesy to offer to pay.

"— one hundred thousand pesos," continued Carmen, "if you come to Santo Poco and put on a show of your strength and stop the . . . the . . . the . . . horrible —" She broke off, searching for words monstrous enough to describe El Guapo's awful villainy.

"Evil . . . murdering . . ." Rodrigo put in helpfully, and Carmen nodded. Good choice.

". . . villainous monster, El Guapo, so that once again we can be a peaceful village." She stopped, satisfied. It was a good message, a strong plea. How could The Three Amigos refuse?

The telegrapher added up the words on his fingers, calculating the cost.

"That'll be twenty-three pesos," he said at last.

Carmen and Rodrigo exchanged horrified looks.

"We . . . we've only got ten," stammered the dismayed girl.

The telegrapher shrugged. "I'll give you the ten-peso

version." Picking up his pencil stub, he began to cross out words as the Sanchez children dumped out their money, every peso they had in the world, and watched anxiously.

He read them the ten-peso version. "You are very great. One hundred thousand pesos to come to Santo Poco, put on show, stop the . . ." The telegrapher stopped for a minute to think. "Horrible, evil, murdering, villainous" — that was four words. One would do. But which one?

"I'll put 'infamous' El Guapo," he told Carmen.

"Infamous?" Her eyebrows shot up; she had never heard the word before.

"It means murderous . . . evil . . . like all you said," the telegrapher assured her. "It'll save you money."

What could the girl say but "Thank you"? They were in God's hands now, God's and the telegraph operator's.

It was over; the die was cast; the key had chattered its mysterious message in Morse code; the telegram had been sent; the fates were on the move; they had done all they could; and there was nothing left to do. Yet the two were reluctant to leave the telegraph office, because their destiny was tied up in that precious message, traveling with such magic fragility over the air through invisible wires.

So they hung around for a few minutes outside the telegraph office, as though The Three Amigos might magically appear. They felt drained, almost let down. Also very, very broke. All they could do now was wait here in Diablo for their heroes to show up, and then the two would lead them back to Santo Poco.

"Now we can only hope that they will come," sighed Carmen.

"They are probably very busy," sighed Rodrigo. There is so much injustice in the world."

But his sister laid a reassuring hand on her brother's thin shoulder. Her face, recalling the unselfish gallantry of The Three Amigos, took on a fresh radiance, and her black eyes sparkled with confidence.

"They will come, Rodrigo," she told him. "They have to come. These men are our only hope."

She sighed again. What great Amigos! What super guys! So handsome! So magnificently dressed! How could they possibly refuse?

Chapter Three

Dawn in Los Feliz, Hollywood, California, always brings the first rays of the blossoming sun slipping silently from the east over the high tops of the date palms and the pink tile roofs of the Spanish-Moorish palaces which rise majestically from the hilly escarpments. High stone walls surrounding tall iron gates give way to avenues of Lombardy poplars. The avenues lead past gently playing sculptured marble fountains up rosy granite steps to massive front doors of crusty oak, deeply carved with lions' heads, and boasting doorknobs as big as basketballs.

Los Feliz's formidable palaces are like a modern-day Mt. Olympus, where one finds a new breed of gods and goddesses — the movie stars, whose silent but expressive faces and dynamic personalities have brought incredible overnight wealth and fame to young men and women who might otherwise have remained vaudeville entertainers, manicurists, shoe clerks, and dance teachers specializing in the Bunny Hop.

In the early days of motion pictures, before the big money moved westward to Bel-Air, Brentwood, and Beverly Hills, Los Feliz, with its castles-in-Spain architecture, half Castilian, half Arabic, was the place to live. Given that fact, dwelling in one of those veritable Alhambras, surrounded by unimaginable opulence and luxury, whom shall we expect to find but our dashing heroes, The Three Amigos?

Dawn brings the milkman, who leaves behind three bottles, each of them golden on top with rising cream, each sealed with a little paper cap wound round with wire. Dawn brings the paperboy, who, balancing on the lowest bar of the forbidding front gate, expertly chucks three copies of the morning edition of the *Los Angeles Eagle* onto the pink granite steps.

Since dawn will not bring any further activity for several hours, and we're likely to be sitting on these stone steps awhile, let's take a look at the front pages of those papers. Once James, the butler, emerges to take them up, they will be folded immediately to the show business pages, and you can kiss good-bye any news of what's happening in the real world.

There's a war on in Europe, and in some obscure place in France, the Somme, a battle is raging that has already been named the bloodiest battle in history; it's been going on for months, involving three million fighting men and an awesome loss of life on both sides. A new weapon called a tank has been deployed at the Somme, but the majority of the casualties are inflicted by the most intensive artillery barrage ever employed in battle.

Here's yet another feature article on that newfangled "theory of relativity" propounded by that crazy scientist Albert Einstein. The theory seem to have two important uses: one, it has formed the basis for some very funny jokes on the Keith-Orpheum vaudeville circuit, and two, it has united mankind in the agreement that nobody except that fuzzy-haired kook professor can understand the first thing about it.

President Wilson is already hot on the trail for re-election, but even as he campaigns on the motto "He kept us out of war," he is hinting that perhaps America should retreat somewhat from her position of neutrality. America in a world war? Forget it! No way!

Oh, oh. Now for the bad news. Somebody named Margaret Sanger has founded the first "birth control clinic," whatever that means. Doesn't sound good. And twenty-four more states have voted Prohibition and gone dry. What the devil is going on here? What with this new cigarette, Lucky Strikes, and this new hot music, jazz, both sweeping across the nation, this noble nation of ours seems to be headed for hell in a handbasket. Thank heaven America still has Edgar Guest, beloved author of *It Takes a Heap o' Livin' to Make a House a Home*. At least some things are still sacred here.

The front door is opening. An impressive figure is emerging. How tall! How handsome! Is it a movie star? No, it's James, the butler. Must be close to ten o'clock. He's bending his august body to pick up the newspapers in his white gloves. Now he's folding the sections back pristinely to those pages which really matter. Hollywood news.

Lots of news today, most of it about Nazimova's big hit, *War Brides*. But here's a story on the filming of D. W. Griffith's *Intolerance*. Every day, seems like Griffith has some feature or other in the paper; he's got to be in tight with the editor, right? How important can this *Intolerance* be? Even if D.W. does claim it's the largest, most costly epic ever filmed, will people stand in line and pay out a hard-earned nickel to watch a movie about religion with half-naked kootch dancers in it? Hmmmmm. You know, that could be . . . educational. . . .

Another western in the movie news — William S. Hart's *Hell's Hinges*. Great title. But Bill Hart is getting on; how much longer can he last? Twenty years? Thirty?

Any news of The Three Amigos? No? Look again. Sure? Oh, well, maybe tomorrow . . . .

The entrance hall soars a full two stories high, with a galleried balcony running around the upper floor. The chandelier alone must weigh a couple of tons of wrought-iron and glass. And those portraits of Spanish grandees — twice as large as life! Whose ancestors are they, hanging in a row in giant baroque gilded frames over a long console table of ormolu-trimmed marble, flanked by thronelike chairs set on griffin's feet? The portraits are reflected across the vast hallway by the largest, heaviest plate-glass mirror money can buy, and the floor is slick terrazzo thinly covered in priceless rugs from Bokhara and Ankara.

Pretty young parlormaids in discreet aprons and frilly caps are tiptoeing through the hallways with fresh linens piled high in their arms, and a liveried footman carries a heavy load of sterling silver through the servants' door to be polished.

James set the folded newspapers down carefully, one each on three silver trays, outside the east-facing dining room, where the blonde and buxom maid, Katrina, has just finished buffing the gold-veined marble floor.

"Are you done with the waxing? The Amigos want that floor sparkling for their party tonight!" The butler looked down critically at the highly polished marble.

"Oh, yes sir!" Katrina's luscious face was quite rosy from exertion, and her breath came in becoming short pants. As did the rest of her. The maid is a humdinger.

"Good," sniffed James. Now, with the deliberate majestic tread that nobody can quite duplicate if not lucky enough to be born an emperor or a butler, he climbed the ornate curved stairway at the end of the soaring entrance hall. Turning to the left, he knocked once discreetly at each of three successive doors, and at each door he left the same firm message.

"Forty minutes to your meeting at the studio with Mr. Flugleman. Breakfast in five minutes."

There was no reply from inside any of the rooms, but

a moment or two later, the first door opened and Ned Nederlander emerged.

Ned was smaller than he looked on screen, and thinner, too. His little pointed face wore a look of constant pained surprise, which changed easily and expressively to either delight or woe, depending on whether you tickled him or stepped on his foot. Ned possessed a neat round head topped by a fluff of soft brown hair, and a childish innocence surrounded him. What Ned Nederlander resembled most was an elegantly dressed twelve-year-old. Under a plaid tweed jacket, which was worn over matching baggy plus fours, as though he were just about to play golf at St. Andrew's, Ned was toting an argyle vest of purest cashmere which went perfectly with the high-topped argyle golfing socks that fitted neatly into his spiked black-and-white shoes.

A split second later, the next door opened and out swept Lucky Day. A long-legged, loose-jointed man with both a shamble and a swagger in his walk, Lucky was, if anything, even more luxuriously dressed than Ned. He sported the latest in masculine fashion, a fuzzy tweed belted jacket, a Norfolk jacket *à l'anglais*, more suited to grouse shooting on the damp, cold Scottish moors than to wearing outdoors in Southern California. He looked even more the sporting Englishman than Ned. Oddly enough, his thick head of hair . . . oops, his head of thick hair . . . which appeared so *yanqui* blond on screen, was actually snowy white.

"Good morning, Lucky," said the first Amigo to the second.

"Good morning, Ned," replied the second Amigo to the first.

"Beautiful day, Lucky."

"Yes, it is, Ned. Beautiful." Neither one had yet taken a step outdoors or had even looked out a window at the sky, but this was Hollywood, California, where all days are equally, impartially, and boringly beautiful.

The sound of the third door slamming on the upstairs landing made the two turn to look. Dusty Bottoms, the third Amigo, was finally putting in an appearance.

Taller than the other two, Dusty possessed an amiable and expressively mobile face distinguished by deep-set eyes, a plump cleft chin, and a ready if somewhat dim-witted smile. Like his Amigos, Dusty, too, was a vision of sartorial splendor, dressed not for golf or grouse shooting, or even for high tea at Buckingham Palace. He was dressed for yachting, in a natty nautical blazer with bright gold buttons and a scarf tucked in at the neck. Creamy white flannel trousers completed the costume. Dusty paused for a moment at the head of the landing to allow his friends to drink in his outfit, then came bounding happily down the stairs to join his Amigos.

Together, The Three Amigos walked down their heavily carpeted stairway, and it was obvious that this perfect morning was not uppermost in their thoughts. Today the Amigos had serious business on their minds and their agendas.

"I have waited three and a half years for this day," stated Lucky as they descended side by side.

Ned's little face took on an anxious expression. "Take it easy with Flugleman today," he cautioned. "Just see if you can get me more real acting moments, where I can show my range as an actor, run the gamut of emotions."

A benign smile crossed Lucky's lips. "You'll get them, Ned, because you deserve them," he promised softly.

"Because you know what, Lucky?"

"What, Ned?"

"That's what's bringing the women into the theater!" declared Ned.

Lucky's face was shadowed as he turned to Dusty. "That's what's bringing the women into the theater," he shrugged. "That's why *I'm* known as 'The Profile.'" He turned his face sideways to let Ned and Dusty get the full benefit of that Roman nose and brow.

"*You* made up being called 'The Profile,'" Dusty pointed out reasonably.

Lucky hadn't the grace to blush, although he did look a little uncomfortable. He kept forgetting how far back The Three Amigos went together, and how well they all knew one another.

"So?" he shrugged. "It's a thing . . . it's working for me. You call yourself 'The Profile' long enough, pretty soon somebody else does, then . . ."

The Amigos had reached the bottom of the curving staircase, and they automatically headed for the foyer mirror, jostling each other as they checked their radiant selves out. Even though it was the largest looking glass Hollywood money could buy, there never seemed to be room in it for more than one Amigo at a time.

Ned treated himself to one of his more flamboyant dramatic gestures, while Lucky, as usual, gazed long and passionately at the celebrated profile. Dusty, who was always satisfied with his reflection, elbowed the other two out of the way he while grinned at his image and smoothed back his dark, lightly curling hair.

"Breakfast is served," announced the imperturbable James.

Now Katrina, an adorable vision in a frilled white cap with little starched white apron to match, came in from the kitchen, carrying a large silver urn of hot coffee on an ornate tray. Under her tight black uniform, her rounded hips swung bewitchingly from side to side.

"Breakfast is served," she echoed redundantly.

There was another jostle as each Amigo determined to enter the dining room first. For one moment all three were jammed tightly and competitively together in the doorway, then little Ned wriggled his wiry body under Lucky's barring arm and dashed across the newly waxed floor, with Lucky Day in pursuit. A race for the chairs ended in a dead heat between the two, while Dusty, the loser, sauntered over casually as if he didn't care. He took his seat with a grin and draped his huge white linen napkin over his lap.

The sideboard was crammed with large silver chafing dishes which kept the food hot. Footmen in livery, wearing immaculate white gloves, passed steaming tureens of scrambled egg, platters of flapjacks buried under golden rivulets of melted butter and sweet syrup, dishes of bacon and sausage and thick slices of country ham half hidden by red-eye gravy. In 1916, cholesterol was a word as yet uncoined.

At each of the places, set with Limoges dishes and heavy sterling flatware, sat a silver tray with a copy of the morning paper, turned to the Hollywood section. Our heroes munched awhile in silence as they scanned the cinema news and sipped strong, scalding coffee out of gold-rimmed Haviland china cups.

"What's Flugleman want to see us about?" asked Dusty at last, swallowing the last of his ham and eggs.

Lucky put down his biscuit. "It's what *we* want to see *him* about," he reminded his Amigo. "We're going to renegotiate our contract with the studio."

Dusty nodded, remembering. "Oh, yeah."

"If there's anything you want, you just let me know," Lucky told him loftily.

"Want?" Dusty's expressive face registered surprise. "Are you kidding? It's great here. The studio gives us this house, our clothes, cars. I love this! I love being a movie star! What more could I want?"

He had a point there. Ned frowned. "Are you sure about this 'renegotiating' thing, Lucky?"

Lucky pushed his chair back from the table for emphasis. "Am I sure about it?" he demanded. "Look, I'm the guy who created The Three Amigos, remember?

Remember back in vaudeville when we were the Arizona Moon Boys, out of work, couldn't get a job, and I said we needed something new and then I looked at us and said . . . 'the three . . .the three. . .'"

"Dusty said 'Amigos,'" Ned reminded him helpfully.

Lucky scowled. Ancient history. He always hated being reminded of that. "Yeah," he was forced to concede, "but I said the 'three' part. That's a very major part. Look, Flugleman fears me." He clenched his jaws and set his fists, or maybe it was the other way around. "He knows I'm a guy who takes what he wants, when he wants it, where he wants it, why he wants it, and who he wants it."

As the other two sat puzzled, trying to figure out that last sentence, Katrina sashayed in from the kitchen, picked up the coffee urn, and sashayed back out again, her round, shapely sashayer moving from side to side like a fleshy metronome.

Three pairs of eyes moved back and forth, back and forth, keeping time with the sinuous rhythm of the parlormaid's hips.

"Excuse me," said Lucky abruptly. "I have to go to the kitchen."

"He's a genius." Dusty shook his head in admiration as Lucky disappeared through the swinging kitchen door. "The man has an intellect of staggering proportions."

"Staggering," agreed Ned, although his voice held less conviction.

In the kitchen, Katrina was keeping herself busy. She was keeping Buster, the chauffeur, busy too. His tongue was halfway down her throat as she tried to get around to the back of him by pushing through his front with her breasts and crotch. It's a good thing that Lucky's new shoes squeaked, or the two servants, caught up in a passionate embrace, wouldn't have heard him soon enough to unglue themselves. As it was, Buster only made it through the back door with a split second to spare, leaving Katrina out of breath and nervously straightening her perky little maid's cap over her mussed hair.

But Lucky didn't notice her dishevelment; his eyes were only for her body, so round, so firm, so tempting . . . so . . . warm. . . . Her high, full breasts felt feverish under her uniform as he clasped them affectionately.

"Katrina, last night —" he began, and broke off, unable to complete the sentence as the heat of her body burned the palms of his hands. His flaring nostrils, however, spoke eloquent volumes. He turned the famous profile so that she could get a real good look at it.

"Yes, yes, it was," breathed Katrina hoarsely, yielding to Lucky's embrace.

"Same time tonight? Eleven-thirty?"

"Yes, tonight," the girl gasped her agreement. "I love you."

"I'll see what's keeping Lucky. We'll be late for our appointment with Flugleman." Ned stood up and walked quickly toward the kitchen.

As the kitchen door swung inward, Lucky let go of Katrina's boobs and the two sprang apart, flushed and panting.

". . . And a little less salt on my morning omelet," he told her sternly.

"Of course, sir. Just as you say."

"That will be all, then." And Lucky strode out, the back of his neck still red.

The moment the door swung closed behind Lucky Day, Ned Nederlander scuttled over to Katrina and grabbed her large breasts in his small hands.

"Last night —" he breathed, stroking and squeezing.

"Incredible!" the maid breathed back.

"Same time tonight? One A.M.?"

"Ohhhh, yesss," moaned Katrina enthusiastically.

Ned smiled impishly. "Tonight it's your turn," he whispered, and the girl rolled her eyes with the anticipation of pleasure. Her turn! Far out!

"Excuse me, Lucky," smiled Dusty, getting up from the table. "I'll just go and see what might be keeping Ned. Wouldn't want to be late for our appointment with Flugleman."

Ned just had time to push Katrina away as the kitchen door swung inward. His face assumed an angry frown, and he raised his voice. ". . . And my shirts should be cleaner, brighter, and have less starch," he instructed the parlormaid, whose cap was now perched below one ear and whose apron had twisted around so that the bow was in the front.

"Yes, sir," she managed to whisper hoarsely as Ned stalked out.

Dusty's hands were fondling her breasts before she had a moment to catch her breath.

"Hmmmm. They're still warm from last night," he purred, making larger circles.

"Only for you," sighed the luscious liar.

"Same time? Three-thirty?"

Katrina opened her mouth to say yes, then stopped. Tonight was going to be *her* turn, and she didn't want to rush it. "Can we make it four?" she purred.

Dusty flashed her the cocky grin for which he was world-famous. "I'll be waiting." Wrapping his long arms around her, he pulled her tightly against him, but a discreet cough at the kitchen door made the two fly apart.

"The car is waiting, sir," said James, imperturbable as always. Katrina's uniform was by now totaled — a rumpled, sweaty mess. Her cap had long ago hit the kitchen floor, and her buttery hair was tumbled over her flushed brow and cheeks, but James never batted an Augustan eyelash. "Your coat, sir," was all he said as Dusty adjusted his trousers.

Dusty followed the butler into the dining room. The other Amigos were already coated, hatted, and waiting.

Silently, the efficient James helped the third Amigo into his outer garment.

Ned Nederlander's scrawny, wiry figure was wrapped in a luxurious overcoat of cashmere, with flaring lapels and a wide belt that tied it bulkily around him. The coat was long enough to hang halfway down to his ankles, at the ends of which winked brightly polished tiny little black shoes. Into the collar of the coat was knotted a fringed scarf of white silk.

Lucky Day's resplendent coat was of alpaca, not cashmere. It was longer, hanging down all the way down to his ankles, and the lapels were a good two inches wider, the encircling sash belt fuller, almost a cummerbund. His scarf, too, was wider, and where Ned's was merely white, Lucky's was a glowing rich maroon.

But, once again, Dusty Bottoms outshone them both. His outfit could be described only as . . . mouth-watering. Yes, mouth-watering was the word for the astounding coat he wore. Not cashmere, not even alpaca, this opulent garment was made of vicuna so thick and so soft that fingers disappeared into it as into the dimpled flesh of a baby's behind. It was as thick as a Persian carpet, as soft as a Persian cat, and big enough to fit two Dustys with room left over for one Ned. Tall as Dusty was (and he was the tallest of the Three Amigos), his coat was taller. Long enough to sweep the floor, the coat seemed to be all lapel and sash; no trousers or shoes peered from underneath. In fact, nothing of Dusty was visible underneath it, except for a glowing glimpse of a glittering scarf of peacock colors that gleamed from around his throat.

Hats. They needed hats. For Lucky, a soft brown felt bowler to match his tweeds. For Ned, a puffy golfing tam of the same plaid as his jacket and plus fours. And for Dusty, a straw skimmer to go with his boating blazer.

They were dressed and ready to go out the front door, which was held open by a footman, then down the long flight of granite steps to the driveway, where the car stood waiting.

This was the real thing; this was what being a movie star was all about. Living in a mansion in Hollywood, California, eating off silver trays, wearing expensive clothing, having an army of servants, including a faithful and affectionate parlormaid at one's disposal day and night, especially night. Driving around in a Hispano-Suiza with snakeskin upholstery in the rumble seat, with a handsome chauffeur to open the doors and tuck you under the lap robe. The car even had fresh flowers in a little cut-glass vase bolted to the door.

Stardom. It was the bee's knees.

Smiling happily and even a little smugly, The Three Amigos drove off in the Hispano to keep their date with destiny. And with Flugleman.

Chapter Four

The suburb of Los Angeles known as Hollywood was not much bigger than a few houses and stores and a couple of dirt roads back in 1916. The tiny town was still surrounded by farms and citrus groves, but it was just beginning to bustle, even though the money men of the motion picture business were snug in their New York offices where the major studios — Vitagraph and Biograph and the others — were flourishing.

About six years earlier, though, the trickle westward to sunny California had begun. The nickelodeons were crying out for more and more product — the moviegoer who plunked down his nickel or his dime wanted more of John Bunny, more of Charlie Chaplin, more of Mary Pickford, more of Mack Sennett's plump and pretty bathing beauties. So film directors and producers went looking for eternal sunshine in which they could shoot movies every day, winter and summer. And they found Hollywood, a dusty little nothingburgh where you could reach up and pick fresh oranges off the trees.

D.W. Griffith was one of the pioneers; he came out first in 1910, then every winter after that for several years, bringing his little band of repertory players, including the beautiful Lillian and Dorothy Gish (D.W. could never tell the sisters apart, so he made them wear different-colored ribbons), on the long train ride west to the sun. In the spring they all went back to New York until one year they simply stayed.

More and more industry people came and stayed, lured by constant sunshine and lower overhead. Cecil B. De Mille built the first film studio in 1913, in a barnlike building they still call The Barn. In The Barn, De Mille shot the first feature film ever made, *The Squaw Man.* It put Hollywood on the map.

Others came, following in C.B.'s footsteps, putting up studios, stages, and even hotels for the actors, who weren't allowed into the better hotels of old Los Angeles. In the beginning, screen actors were considered trash. A few years later, they would be worshipped as gods.

Among the first studios built in Hollywood was Goldsmith Productions. Busy and wealthy, it had grown to a vast complex, standing out on La Brea very close to the tar pits, right over the fossilized dinosaur bones. The land was cheap; ironically, sixty years later oil would be discovered on the property, and that handful of acres of oozy ground would be worth a fortune, bringing more money flowing in inside a month than all the Goldsmith film productions put together had earned in a lifetime. But that was in the future.

There had once been a real Goldsmith of Goldsmith Productions, a former furrier who had, like so many others, wandered into the brand-new business of motion pictures quite by accident. A combination of good luck and bad taste had made him immediately successful; as the nickels and dimes from the box offices had mounted into great piles, Isidore Goldsmith's ideas had become more grandiose; he demanded that his pictures be Artistic, no more of the boobs and the bellylaffs. "Give me Art!"

he cried. At the same time, he began to gamble heavily, first on games of pinochle, then on poker, horses, and anywhere else he could lose a dollar. Caught between artistic motion pictures with no audiences and the gambling losses of its founder, Goldsmith Productions, with multiple standing sets, opulent dressing rooms, and impressive executive offices, began to lose money. Soon it was ripe for takeover.

Enter Harry Flugleman.

Like Goldsmith and so many others, Flugleman had come into the movie business by the back door. Arriving steerage class in the United States from a tiny *shtetl* in western Russia, where the Flugleman family was accustomed to starving, freezing, or being knocked off by the pogroms, Heschl Flugleman (he would become Harry as soon as he learned to speak English) carried with him a dream of success and power, all to be fueled by enormous wealth. Where the wealth was supposed to come from, he had no idea. Yet. But he was only twenty years old, and filled with a ferocious energy.

Flugleman went to work as a pants presser. But he was a smart pants presser. Living on almost nothing a week, eating day-old rye bread from the cheapest bakery, Harry lent out the few pennies he earned . . . at sizable interest. By the time he was twenty-four, Harry had enough money amassed to quit pants pressing, but he didn't. He continued to slave over the ironing board while his money went to work all over the city, growing every week.

When the money had grown big enough to buy a tenement building, he bought one. Harry Flugleman became a landlord. Soon he owned a sizable chunk of the Lower East Side, including a crummy little nickelodeon which rented space in one of his buildings. The nickelodeon manager drank, and his employees stole him blind; when he couldn't pay his rent, Flugleman foreclosed and was now the owner of a theater that showed one- and two-reel comedies at three-cents-a-head admission.

While he was deciding what to do with the space, Harry

put his cousin Schmul in charge of the nickelodeon; Schmul was too religious to drink and too dumb to steal. Soon the money began coming in, even at only three cents a head. Pennies piled up into respectable dollars.

Flugleman was astonished. Here was something new, a business with a tiny overhead, almost no investment, and look! Pure profit! This required closer examination. It soon became clear to him that the real money was not in showing the product, but in supplying it. Give the people what they want and they'll stand in line in the rain, with their four pennies (Flugleman had raised the price of admission) clutched tightly and happily in their hands. On that fateful day when recognition dawned, Harry Flugleman, landlord, turned into Harry Flugleman, film producer. He determined to acquire a studio of his own before he was forty years old.

Within three years he had almost realized his dream, pushing Isidore Goldsmith out the gates of the studio he'd founded and taking over as studio head, although he was still nominally responsible to the money men in New York. But give him time. . . . Someday . . .

Flugleman's idea of films was crude but effective — the public wanted action, laughter, tears, and tits. Give it to them. The only thing left standing of Isidore Goldsmith's dream of Art was his name over the studio gates and the motto, *Arte Perire Sua*, carved over the studio portals by a stonemason with a cynical nature and a mordant sense of humour. It's a good thing that nobody could read Latin, because the motto didn't say what Goldsmith thought it said, although the word "Arte" had reassured him.

It was through these very gates and under the carved motto that the Hispano-Suiza drove majestically, ferrying The Three Amigos. Once inside the studio gates, however, Dusty, Lucky, and Ned descended from the haughty limousine and walked, partly to see and greet the other movie stars, who were strolling down the studio alleyways in full costume, but mostly to be seen and be greeted themselves, as Goldsmith Productions' triple-threat stellar attraction.

The Amigos strode confidently across the studio lot, scattering greetings to their fellow players. Those higher-paid stars of great rank and bigger billing than our three didn't bother to wave or smile; those receiving lower pay and lower billing responded eagerly to the Amigos' hellos. But that was the etiquette around the studio, around Hollywood, and in fact around most of the civilized world.

A busty blonde laced tightly into a Marie Antoinette costume was waving and yoo-hooing at The Three Amigos, but Lucky hissed through his teeth, "Don't look. It's Miss Renee," and the three of them marched past without turning their heads. If there was anybody they loathed, it was Miss Renee, the ersatz European who had been foisted upon them as the love interest in their newest movie, *Those Darn Amigos*.

On the stucco wall of the studio, just outside the executive building, was posted a three-sheet billboard announcing The Three Amigos' latest film. There they were, almost as large as life, grinning in top hat and tails, with Luck Day's profile very much in evidence. The credit line on the poster read, *Those Darn Amigos, featuring Miss Renee*. At their own images, the three of them smiled; at Miss Renee's, they scowled. Imitation French trollop! Tasteless tart! How they despised her!

The inevitable rooting section of faithful fans and autograph seekers was hanging around as usual, hoping for a glimpse of their heroes. Graciously, Lucky, Ned, and Dusty signed autographs and smiled their famous photogenic smiles. Making their fans happy was the part of the business they loved the best — that and the money and the house and the cars and the servants and the fine clothes. Also, they got off on the cheers and waves that followed their progress into the executive building.

Inside, at the nerve center of the studio, Mr. Flugleman's

marble-floored, expensively furnished office was humming with activity. Flugleman himself was in the grip of one of his fits of commercial genius.

He was pacing back and forth on his marble floor, while his yes-man, Morty, stood by ready to carry out or relay his orders. Morty had a yes-man of his own, Sam, who put Mr. Flugleman's commands through instantly to other underlings. Flugleman told Morty what to do, and Sam did it. He was always at the telephone, a large, shiny black two-handed affair, with separate earpiece and mouthpiece linked by a cord.

"Streamlining!" declared Flugleman. "That's the word today!" He stopped to take a Havana cigar out of a silver-rimmed humidor, and Morty instantly leapt forward to light it. "Streamline the art department! Streamline the legal department! Streamline the music department! Streamline props! Streamline costumes!"

Immediately Sam began to bark instructions into the phone, yelling "Streamline!" to whatever flunky was on the other end of the wire. Sam had no idea what the hell he was talking about, but Mr. Flugleman signed the checks, so Mr. Flugleman's word was law.

But Morty looked puzzled. That was part of his job, to look puzzled until Flugleman explained his brilliant ideas, then to applaud enthusiastically. "Streamlining, Mr. Flugleman?"

Flugleman scowled, although he was pleased by the question. "Those guys in New York think we sit around all day pulling our puds. They think I don't know how to run a studio? They think I don't know how to trim our sails? How to separate the wheat from the chaff?"

Morty looked even more confused. What did sails or wheat have to do with motion pictures? Was Flugleman planning a sea epic? Was the wheat supposed to be the cargo?

Harry Flugleman pounded one manicured fist on his vast polished desk. He was a middle-sized, not yet middle-aged man, dressed nattily in a vested business suit. A gold watch chain with several fobs stretched across the protuberance of his little round belly. The thick dark hair on his head was just beginning to be touched with a silvery gray, which Flugleman considered distinguished.

"Goldsmith Productions is going to make *people* movies, Morty. Movies about people, made by people, with people in them that people want to see."

No doubt about it, the man was a cinematic genius, a veritable Einstein.

"Makes a lot of sense, Mr. Flugleman," Morty agreed promptly, while Sam began yelling into the phone, "More people movies!"

Without knocking, Flugleman's secretary, Nancy, a trim, efficiently pretty girl, walked in.

"They just called from the gate, sir," she announced. "The Three Amigos are on their way up to see you."

Flugleman scowled, and his jet-black eyebrows drew together on either side of his cigar. "We'll be just a minute. Have them wait," he instructed. "Morty, what are we doing with The Three Amigos?"

"Sandy and Irving are working on something where The Three Amigos meet Cochise."

"Uh-huh," the studio boss grunted. "Their last picture . . . uh . . ." He struggled briefly and vainly with his memory for the name of the film, then snapped his fingers.

"Those Darn Amigos," his yes-man supplied immediately. The scowl deepened, and the cigar vibrated in annoyance as memory returned. Flugleman shook his head. "That was a big mistake. Too sophisticated. Not enough of a people picture." Then the scowl lightened as the tycoon's face softened. A tiny smile played around the cigar.

"Miss Renee was swell in it, don't you think, Morty?"

"Best thing in the picture, Mr. Flugleman," answered Morty promptly.

"Best thing in the picture," echoed Sam.

Flugleman's eyes began to glow as the smile widened; the studio chief was looking positively dreamy.

"She's a beautiful woman, Morty," he said softly.

You oughtta know. But out loud, Morty replied with fervor, "She certainly is, Mr. Flugleman."

"She's going to be a big star."

"I'm sure of it." *How could she help it? She's certainly going about it in the right way.*

"You know, Morty, the studio has a lot of money tied up in Miss Renee."

Yes, and most of it's on her back. Well, why not? That's where she earned it, on her back. "And she's worth every penny of it, Mr. Flugleman."

Suddenly the dreamy smile faded, and Flugleman was all business again. The cigar, always a barometer, pointed straight forward. "Morty, we got to watch the budget on this Cochise picture. This movie is the Amigos' last chance."

"We've already streamlined it." His aide nodded. "We're gonna take the boys down to Baja and shoot the picture in eight days."

The studio head's fist banged the big desk again, but this time in approval. "Great. Streamlining. That's the ticket, Morty."

Announced by Nancy, the secretary, The Three Amigos sauntered into the inner office of Harry Flugleman. The first few times they had seen it they were struck by the absolute magnificence of the place. Studios had come a long way in the three years since De Mille had built The Barn. Flugleman's office was palatial, the painted ceiling with its stained-glass insets held up by heavy columns of malachite, themselves topped by acanthus finials picked out in genuine gold leaf. Tall potted palms stood around in rare Chinese vases from the T'ang Dynasty. The floors were a complicated inlaid mosaic of the finest Italian travertine gold-flecked marble. Flugleman's desk had been recovered from a seventeenth century sunken Spanish galleon, and was constructed of the finest mahogany, with a gold-tooled leather top.

On the other side of the vast room, a large ducal escutcheon, "liberated" from the set of *The Castle of Farnsworth* when that film had wrapped, ornamented the far wall. Although Harry Flugleman had never actually claimed that the escutcheon represented his own family's coat of arms, he had never actually denied it, either.

Yet by now, impressive and imposing though the office was, the boys had become accustomed to it and took its opulence for granted. They felt very much at home, and entered laughing and confident, giving everybody the glad hand. After all, were they not The Three Amigos, indispensable to Goldsmith Productions and its profit picture?

Flugleman, however, did not respond to the glad-handing. As usual, he wanted to concentrate only on business.

"Now, here's the way I see it," he began almost at once. "We've strayed with you guys. We went away from the formula. We've got to get back to basics. *Shootin' for Love, Wanderers of the West, The Ride of The Three Amigos* — all the great Amigo pictures had one thing in common. Three wealthy Spanish landowners who fight for the rights of the peasants. That's something everybody loves. It's a people idea. It's a story a nation can sink its teeth into. Then came *Those Darn Amigos*. A box office failure. Nobody went to see it because nobody cares about three wealthy Spanish landowners on a weekend in Manhattan! We strayed from the formula and we paid the price!" Flugleman chomped furiously on his cigar.

There was a moment's stunned silence, then Ned said, with wounded dignity, "I thought we were quite good in it."

"Good?" exclaimed Lucky. "We were great."

"Unfortunately," Dusty added helpfully, "we were forced to play second fiddle to that French cow."

Sam and Morty gasped in horror, and Flugleman's eyes narrowed. He bit down viciously on the doomed cigar. "Were you speaking about Miss Renee?" he inquired quietly, too quietly.

But The Three Amigos, caught up in their own mystique, failed to read the warning signs, the thunderclouds gathering over the studio head's brow.

"Yeah, the 'Oops' girl," giggled Ned, cracking up the other two. Nudging one another in the ribs, the three broke into a cacophony of cow noises and other, ruder, anatomical sounds, at the same time holding their noses and pantomiming "stinko."

"Tell the boys about the Cochise picture, Morty." Sam hastened to change the dangerous subject.

"Sandy and Irving are working on it right now. You meet Cochise. At first you think he's a terrible guy. You fight, then you get to know him, you come to respect each other, and at the end of the picture, you're friends." Morty glanced at the Amigos to check out their reaction to the scenario, but there was none. They remained stone-faced.

"We send you boys down to Baja and we shoot the picture in eight days," put in Flugleman. "What do you think?"

Lucky glanced at his two companions for confirmation, then took a step forward. "That'll be the day."

"What did he say?" snapped Flugleman.

"He said, 'That'll be the day,' Mr. Flugleman," echoed Morty.

Wheeling around angrily, Flugleman bit his cigar in two. "What!" he exclaimed.

"I don't think you understand who you're talking to here," continued Lucky, oblivious to the wrath. "We've got a few items to straighten out first, or there might be three actors who don't really feel like making a Geronimo picture."

"What the hell are you talking about?!" demanded Flugleman.

Ned took one frightened little hopping step backward. Suddenly reading Flugleman's face and tone, he had an instant mental picture of three Amigos standing on the brink of disaster with one toe over the line.

"Lucky, I think we ought to back off," he said anxiously in a loud stage whisper.

But there was no stopping Lucky Day when he was on a roll. He just barreled along, looking neither right nor left, not even stopping to take a breath. "What we're talking about is money," he stated arrogantly. "Real Money. Amigo money. No dough, no show."

The contorted lips of an enraged Harry Flugleman spit out the fragments of his dead cigar, and Ned's heart sank. But Lucky noticed nothing. He was unstoppable.

"Plus, I see a new type of movie for the Amigos. No more of these people-type movies. . . ."

"Yeah," interrupted Dusty, trying to look authoritative. "Much less streamlining."

"Boys, boys," began Mr. Flugleman. "Let me say just one thing . . ." Now he broke into a roar of rage. "IT'LL BE A COLD DAY IN HELL BEFORE HARRY FLUGLEMAN LETS AN ACTOR TELL HIM WHAT TO DO!" he screamed, the pulsing veins standing out in his forehead. "You know what the word *nada* means?" he demanded. "In all those Mexican movies you made, did you ever hear that word?"

Dusty racked his brains. "Is it a light chicken gravy?"

A low growl escaped from Flugleman's throat and suddenly cold, wet realization like last week's flounder hit the other two Amigos smack between the eyes. Now, too late, Lucky and Dusty finally perceived what Ned had already seen: that perhaps not as many options were open to The Three Amigos as they'd believed. Perhaps a little fancy backtracking footwork was in order here. Lucky cleared his throat.

But Flugleman took no notice; he was too angry. "It means NOTHING!" he shrieked. "Zero! Zip! It's what you're going to have when I'm through with you. You hit Harry Flugleman on a bad day!"

Dusty Bottoms turned a little green and smiled a sickly smile. "I'd like to continue to work for free, Mr. Flugleman," he gurgled.

"Are you living in the studio mansion?" barked the studio chief.

"Yeah, but . . ." began Lucky.

Flugleman cut him off. "Well, not anymore you're not! Morty, move Miss Renee into the studio mansion!"

"The Amigos are out of the mansion. Miss Renee is in," Sam snapped into the phone.

"Out of the mansion?" squeaked Dusty in disbelief.

"They have cars and drivers, too, Mr. Flugleman," offered Morty helpfully.

"You stay out of this," snarled Lucky, but it was already past saving.

"Get rid of their cars!" ordered Flugleman and, "No more cars for the Amigos," Sam instructed the telephone.

Now Harry Flugleman's furious eye fell on the snazzy outfits the boys were sporting. "Where'd you get those clothes?" he snarled. "From a movie?"

"Yeah," replied Ned nervously. "The studio *gave* them to us. *Those Darn Amigos.*"

"Well, we're takin' them back. Morty!"

"Gotcha, Mr. Flugleman," Sam responded. Into the phone, he ordered, "Get wardrobe over here right away. Take the Amigos' clothes."

"Wait a minute!" Ned protested. "You can't take our clothes! You *gave* us these clothes! They were presents!" But almost before the words had left his lips, six wardrobe people had appeared and were dragging the clothes off the Amigos' struggling bodies. The tweed Norfolk suit, the boating blazer, the plaid golfing outfit were all bundled up and carried away in the space of less than a minute.

The Three Amigos stood there, not only horrified but in their underwear. All that was left to them was shirts and drawers, socks and garters and their hats, although Ned seemed to have hung on to his necktie and Lucky to his spats. This was like some horrible dream come true! In only one indiscreet moment, one stupid little flash of time, one blitheringly idiotic, moronic, dimwitted, cretinous, brainless eyeblink they had lost it all — Katrina, stardom, the house, their jobs, their cars, their servants, and their pants!

Yet Lucky was still undaunted; something might still be salvaged if he didn't lose his nerve.

"Hey, hang on here a second! I think you misread who you're talking to!" he yelled with as much conviction as he could muster.

"Misread!" hollered the exasperated Flugleman. "I want these schmucks off my lot! Your asses have just been streamlined. The Three Amigos are history!"

As if by magic, three burly security guards appeared and laid hands on our heroes, hustling them out of the office over their scuffling protests. Ungently they were propelled into the street and ungently bounced onto the sidewalk, right by the studio gates.

The nightmare was growing blacker and more unbearable by the minute. As the three stood there in their underwear and socks, they watched with horror as their poster was ripped off the studio wall, while a full-length shot of Miss Renee in her Marie Antoinette outfit was being pasted up in its place. The fickle fans who had cheered them so lustily on their triumphant arrival now stood silent and disapproving at their undignified departure. Worse yet, they began ripping the Amigos' once-treasured autographs out of their books, shredding them to the winds. Nightmare on top of nightmare!

"You had to do it!" Ned flung bitter reproaches in Lucky's teeth. "You had to say it! You had to tell Flugleman how to make movies."

"Flugleman doesn't mean this," Lucky countered, in shock, his confidence ebbing, but still in the fight. "It's a ploy. He knows I know movies. You guys don't understand the business. I've been in the business since I was three!"

Ned laughed sourly. "You're a profile, all right, a profile in stupidity! This is all your fault!"

"My fault?" gasped Lucky. "*My* fault?! I was just looking out for *you* guys!"

His eyes brimming over, little Ned bit his lip to keep the tears back. "We've lost our house, our cars, our clothes . . ." He broke off, not trusting himself to continue without breaking down.

"Mr. Flugleman said not to let them back in for anything," the security guard instructed the gate watchman as he hustled the Amigos outside.

Like Adam and Eve being expelled from the garden of Eden by a flaming sword, The Three Amigos watched helplessly as the gates of their paradise slammed in their faces, leaving them on the wrong side.

"So this is what being dead is like," said Ned softly, half to himself.

Dusty, the eternal optimist, fished around a minute, looking for something to make them all feel better, and came up with a gem. "You know, Mr. Flugleman paid us a real nice compliment in there."

"What was that?" spit out Lucky.

"He said we were history."

Ned's little face crumpled in mingled desperation and exasperation. "What are we going to do? We can't just stand around here in our unmentionables!"

Lucky turned on his famous Lucky grin, and held up his hands, palms up. "Boys, I know the movie business," he reassured them. "Something always turns up."

As if on cue, a messenger boy in a Western Union uniform and cap came riding up on a bicycle.

"Telegram for The Three Amigos," he announced, placing the little yellow envelope into Lucky's upturned palm.

See-what-did-I-tell-you? said Lucky's eyebrows as he tore open the envelope and scanned the message.

"Three Amigos, Hollywood, California," he read out loud: "'You are very great. One hundred thousand pesos to come to Santo Poco . . .'"

"A hundred thousand?" gasped Ned and Dusty in chorus.

"'. . . Put on show, stop the in-famous El Guapo . . .'"

"'In-famous . . .'" Dusty's amiable face was clouded by a puzzled frown. "That's like when a guy is . . . uh . . . what is that? What does that mean?"

Ned's rich peal of laughter was tinged with scornful pity. "Oh, Dusty," he chortled. "In-famous is like when someone is more than famous. This man El Guapo is not just *famous*, he's *infamous*." It was so simple, but then, so was Dusty.

Dusty shook his head, less than completely convinced by Ned's explanation. "I think I've heard of him," he began doubtfully, but Lucky interrupted, his face radiant with confidence, an enthusiastic grin lighting up his features.

"A hundred thousand pesos to do a single personal appearance with this guy El Guapo, who is probably the biggest star to ever come out of Mexico!" Lucky's confidence was rapidly returning.

Now Ned Nederlander had caught Lucky's enthusiasm. "We go down, fire our guns, ride around a little, make a little noise, get the hundred thousand dollars, and we're back in a week." His eyes sparkled at the thought of so much money.

"That's pesos, Ned," said Lucky.

"Dollars, pesos, what difference does it make?" Dusty shrugged. "It's money."

Dusty was right; it was time for action. "Let's go home and get our stuff," suggested Lucky, and the other two Amigos nodded. Who said The Three Amigos were finished, washed up? Whoever it was, they'd show him!

Chapter Five

It was a sorry-looking trio that shambled back to Los Feliz on foot and in underwear, a very different little group from the one that had started out so many long hours ago beautifully dressed and in chauffeur-driven luxury. By the time they reached what they still thought of as "Amigo Mansion," Lucky, Dusty, and Ned were limping, sweating, thirsty, exhausted, and embarrassed. On the long trek home from the studio, there had been too many witnesses to their humiliation, too many jeering fingers had been pointed at them, too many horselaughs had been enjoyed at their expense.

Out of breath, The Three Amigos scrambled up the marble steps and beat on the heavy door. It opened, and the imperturbable face of James, the patrician butler, stared down at them with no recognition.

"May I help you?"

"James, it's us!" cried Lucky.

The butler didn't blink an eyelash. "Yes, I see it is.

But I'm afraid that Mr. Flugleman left orders that you were not to enter the house."

"We just want our stuff. Our clothes," said Dusty.

"All your things are studio property," returned James.

"James, we don't have a change of clothes!" Ned was practically sobbing.

"That's not my concern, Master Ned."

"James! For old-times' sake," implored Ned. "You've known me since I was Little Neddy Knickers. We're practically family!"

"I'm sorry, Master Ned," the butler said firmly, and slammed the door in the Amigos' faces.

The boys looked at one another in horror and began to beat on the door again. An angry voice from above made them look up. Dressed in a satin negligee over a lace-trimmed nightgown, the despised Miss Renee — the "Oops" girl — was scowling down at them from a small stone balcony outside what used to be Lucky's bedroom.

"What the hell is going on out here?" she shrieked. It was evident from her delicate tones that the closest Miss Renee had ever come to her native France was a bouillabaisse restaurant on the Coney Island pier.

"Miss Renee . . . we came to . . ." Dusty began.

"You came to the end of the road, boys," she laughed nastily. "*I'm* living here now. Harry wants it that way. Youse guys are trespassing, so get the hell outta here before I call Harry!"

"We need our clothes!" pleaded Lucky. "Our Amigos costumes."

Miss Renee threw back her fluffy blonde head and uttered a shrill, triumphant laugh. "You're too late. They came and got everything this afternoon, and took all your crap back to the studio. Now buzz off, I've got a big scene tomorrow. *I'm* still working."

And with another evil chuckle, she disappeared off the balcony.

That fried their bacon to a crisp. Not only wasn't there

any justice, there seemed to be no mercy, either. If they couldn't get their hands on their Amigos costumes, how could they keep that one-day easy play date in Santo Poco that would earn them all that money? What they needed was a plan. . . .

It was Lucky, a born leader, who came up with the plan. It wasn't a complicated plan, but it would be murder to carry out. Yet what other choice had they? All they had to do was to break into the studio, which was locked and guarded, then break into the locked and presumably guarded costume department in the wardrobe building and steal . . . er, that is, borrow . . . their Amigos outfits.

"But how do we get into the studio?" demanded Ned plaintively.

"Easy," grinned Lucky. "We go over the wall."

"But it's nine or ten feet high!" protested Dusty.

"Look, I'll go first," explained Lucky. "You two boost me up onto the top of the wall. I'll take a rope with me for getting you up and lowering us down the other side. Then, if the coast is clear, I'll lower the rope and do a birdcall, and you guys come up. It's no big deal."

"Not for you, maybe," pointed out Ned. "You're handy with a rope. It's your stock in trade. Me, I'm an actor, not a cat burglar."

"If you intend to *stay* an actor, then we've got to get hold of those costumes in order to get hold of those pesos," Lucky retorted. "It's our only chance. Unless, of course, you'd rather go back to vaudeville. Four shows a day, six on Saturday, 'Funny Fellows, Comical Song and Dance a Specialty.' Remember Duluth? We died in Duluth. You wanna play Duluth again?"

Ned Nederlander sighed. "I guess not. I suppose we have no choice."

"Now you're talking. Just keep that thought right up there simmering on the front burner of your memory. No choice."

"Are you sure it wouldn't be easier just to go to Flugleman and ask him for our Amigos costumes?" asked Dusty. He and Ned were scrunched down at the base of the studio wall, their hearts in their mouths. It was dark, and only the dim illumination cast by a nearby streetlamp shed any light on their perilous situation. Security police were all over the studio, especially at night.

Ned shook his head. "Are you serious? Flugleman *hates* us right now, thanks to ; . ." He gestured above his head to the top of the wall, where Lucky had been boosted up only a minute or two before. "He's not going to give us our costumes. Lucky's right. This is the only way."

The rope came down suddenly. "Tweet tweet," sounded above their heads. Lucky's signal.

"I don't know," sighed Dusty unhappily. "This is illegal."

"Tweet tweet!"

"Not if you're stealing costumes that fit only you," rationalized Ned. "Besides, think of the money. A hundred thousand pesos. . . ."

"TWEET TWEET!! TO WHIT . . . TO WHOOOOO!!!"

"Yeah," nodded Dusty, feeling better. "That's a whole buncha pesos, isn't it?"

"COCK A DOODLE DOOOOOO!!!" There was a loud whirring noise, exactly as though an Amigo were standing on top of a wall flapping his arms like a crazy crane. "WHOOOOOO, WHOOOOOOOOO!!" whooped the crazy crane.

"Yes, it is," replied Ned. "Wonder how Lucky's doing?"

As if on cue, Lucky yelled down in exasperation, "Hey, you guys! Come on!"

Dusty and Ned stood up and walked around the wall.

"How'd you get in?" asked Lucky in astonishment as he lowered himself down the rope with some effort and joined the other two on the ground.

"Gate was open," answered Dusty.

"Oh. Okay, let's go."

They set out stealthily, running silently on their toes, keeping as close as possible to the sheltering wall, and vanishing into the shadows whenever they spotted a studio guard. Soon they had reached the central square across from the cluster of buildings past the shooting stages.

"There's the wardrobe building," whispered Lucky. "We'll go across one at a time, okay?" The other two Amigos nodded.

"Okay, now!" At the signal, all three dashed forward at once. They had practically reached the wardrobe building when they ground to a screeching halt, realizing that Lucky's orders had somehow been disobeyed. Accordingly, they trooped back across the open square to the shelter of the executive building.

"I said one at a time!" barked Lucky.

Ned dropped his eyes sheepishly. "You were looking right at me. I thought you meant me first."

Dusty raised a stubborn chin. "When you two went, what was I suppose to do, stand here?"

"I'll go first," Lucky told them.

"Who should go second?" asked Dusty.

Lucky shrugged impatiently. "I don't care. You two work it out." Looking both ways, he dashed across the open area and made it safely to the wardrobe building. Straightening up, he waited for the other Amigos to join him. And waited. And waited. No sign of them. After a minute, there was nothing else to do but dash back.

Ned and Dusty were still safe in the shadows; they hadn't moved a step.

"What are you *doing*?" demanded Lucky.

"We're still working it out," Dusty said.

"Goddamn it!" Lucky lost his temper. "We'll go as a clump!" He darted forward once more, alone, and the other two followed in single file. One by one, they arrived safely at the wardrobe building.

"Sorry," apologized Dusty in answer to Lucky's glare. "I didn't know what you meant by a clump."

"I didn't hear you at all," said Ned.

Lucky shook his head. "Forget it. Ned, try the window."

The window was open. They climbed inside.

The wardrobe building was a vast storehouse, dark and crowded to the high ceilings with cinema history. Costumes of every description hung on racks or were stacked against the walls. There were Indian bows and arrows and lances; frontiersmen's rifles and buckskins; satin and lace court dress from the era of Louis the Sun King; Pilgrim buckled hats and colonial buckled shoes; gorilla costumes with hairy staring masks. Only a few low-wattage night lights had been left on; their dim illumination cast weird, menacing shadows on the walls and the ceilings. It was one spooky place to find yourself in, especially in the dead of night. But they didn't dare to turn on any lights, not with guards patrolling the studio lot outside.

"Watch the armor," warned Lucky as the three of them picked their way across the hodgepodge of costumes and props.

Too late. A heavy steel suit of fifteenth century armor went down with a resounding crash as Dusty the klutz knocked it over. As the metallic racket died away slowly, The Three Amigos stopped dead, frozen, waiting to see if anybody outside had heard the noise and was coming on the run. Nothing.

"Dusty, see if you can find the guns," ordered Lucky.

"Here they are," called Ned from a few feet farther on. He held up one of the pearl-handled silver-plated six-shooters.

"Hey, here's some blanks!" Dusty yelled from the stacks.

"Take the whole box," commanded Lucky. "We're going to need them for the show." Dusty nodded and tucked the box of harmless blank cartridges under his arm.

Up ahead, Ned Nederlander had stopped in his tracks,

a look of wonder and excitement shining on his little face. "There they are," he said in a reverent half whisper.

The other two approached silently, with awed footsteps, until they reached Ned's side. Then reverence softened their faces as well.

There they were indeed — the fabled costumes of the legendary Three Amigos. They had been placed on dressmakers' dummies, and a glowing radiance emanated from them as though these glorious suits possessed heroic lives of their own.

Lucky reached up and took his bowler hat off slowly, holding it to his chest. His eyes never left the costumes.

"My God, they're so beautiful," whispered Ned.

"I never thought I'd see them again," whispered Dusty.

"Let's get 'em, boys," whispered Lucky.

Without speaking, they removed the clothing from the dummies and began to dress, handling their costumes with loving respect. It was a ritual robing, rather like that of a knight before a tournament or a matador before a corrida.

The ruffled shirts went on first, then the wide-legged pants; cummerbunds were tightened around their waists; short jackets, rich with silver-thread embroidery, were pulled over shoulders and smoothed down over chests; boots were tugged up and silver spurs fastened; gunbelts were strapped on and buckled with fancy buckles; and the heavy six-guns holstered. Finally, the sombreros, wide and heavy, were placed over their brows, one sombrero over each brow.

No longer were these men merely Lucky Day, Dusty Bottoms, and Ned Nederlander. Here stood The Three Amigos in all their glory. They looked smarter, they looked tougher. They even looked taller, or maybe it was only the sombreros.

Ned twirled his guns with a flourish. "I must admit, it feels pretty good," he grinned.

But before the others could reply, lights snapped on, and four night watchmen, alerted when the suit of armor hit the ground with a mighty crash and rattle, burst in the door.

"Hey, what the hell is going on here?"

"Let's go, Amigos!" shouted Lucky.

At once, the trio swung into action. As the guards came pounding toward them, guns drawn, the Amigos seized ropes that hung conveniently overhead. With one graceful movement, they went flying through the air, their booted feet knocking down guards like ninepins as they swung. With new momentum, they swung again, this time through the wide wardrobe building window, dropping like agile cats to the studio lot below.

They were not alone. A swarm of guards was out searching the grounds.

"Come on this way. . . ." whispered Lucky, and he led the way, disappearing into the shadows, followed by Ned and Dusty, the latter keeping the precious box of blank bullets tightly under his arm.

They moved tightly together now, a team, no longer the ragged little group of incompetents, but a lean, mean machine, born to ride, fight, and love. The Three Amigos, that's who they were, and they knew it. With skill and daring, they eluded their pursuers, who went tripping over their own feet as our heroes ran circles around them, always just out of reach, eluding them, tantalizing them, taunting them. At last they reached the studio walls, just by the front gate.

No doubt the gate was still open, but The Three Amigos didn't choose to find out. In a matter of seconds, they had climbed the wall easily and without a rope. Now they stood on the pinnacle, laughing down at the frustrated guards. Taking off their sombreros, The Three Amigos waved them merrily. Then, moving as one, they executed the famous Three Amigos salute — one, two: hands crossed on chest; three: hands on hips.

Before the guards could move to follow, the three had disappeared into the night. Now on to Santo Poco, to keep their engagement with the in-famous actor El Guapo. The show must go on!

Chapter Six

The Tubbman 601 came circling slowly down out of the sky like a big lazy buzzard. Its canvas-covered fuselage and stubby biplane wings gave it the appearance of a flying laundry bag, but in 1916 it was as high-tech as a Phantom jet, only rarer. Flying machines were not something one saw every day, except over the trenches and battlefields of France. This was the first airship ever to land in the desert just outside of Diablo, Mexico. If the Diablans had known of it, the entire population of the little border town would have turned out to see this marvel touch down. But they didn't, so the desert was empty, except for a Joshua tree or two and some prickly pear cactus.

With no one to see him or gasp in astonishment, a strongly built man dressed in flying leathers stepped down from the aeroplane. His appearance was worth a gasp. There was something about him that said more plainly than words, "Don't mess around with me," or, rather, "Don't mess around vit me," because he was a German.

His leather jacket fit snugly across his muscular chest, and his leather helmet covered the fact that his hair was cropped so short that his skull looked shaven. When he pushed the goggles up onto his brow, the Diablans might have seen (had they been present) another marvel — a crescent-shaped dueling scar slashed across his left cheek. This saber cut was the mark of the Heidelberg University student just as a blue athletic sweater with a white Y was the mark of the American Yalie. And both were worn with equal pride.

Hanging low on his hips in a gunbelt, the German wore a pair of pearl-handled six-guns, western weapons, not European. They contrasted strongly with the military cut of his leather clothing, but the German wore them easily and naturally, exactly at the level of his hands for a rapid draw. Even so, there was something very foreign about his entire appearance; in this ragtag and bobtail frontier town that had seen them all, the German stood out.

Stretching to get the aches out of his shoulder and neck muscles, the German walked stiffly, his back ramrod straight, into the town of Diablo. He made straight for the Cantina del Borrachos, and pushed his way in through the swinging doors. At once, every eye was upon him, and the desperadoes at the bar whispered to one another, chuckling under their breath. This dude's fancy leather getup struck them as ridiculous, a perfect target for their derision.

"Do you haff any beer?" the German inquired of the bartender.

"Just tequila."

The other nodded and took a sip of the raw, noxious drink the bartender set before him. Then he asked in a whisper, "I am looking for a man called El Gvapo. Do you know dis man?"

The men at the bar snickered at the German's mispronunciations, but the bartender only answered carefully, "Perhaps, señor."

Behind him, the same gringo bandit who'd tried to kiss Carmen said out loud, "Do you haffff any beer?" in a rough mimicry of the German's accent.

"El Gvapo vill be anxious to see me. I haff somezing he vants."

This occasioned more guffaws, and the gringo called out, "Hey, where'd you get them purty little guns? Hey, Ah'm talkin' to you! Where did you get them guns?"

But the German chose to ignore the insult and didn't bother to turn around. He continued to speak only to the bartender. "I am meeting some friends of mine here. Zey are coming in on ze afternoon stagecoach. Ven zey arrive, tell zem to vait."

"How will I know them?" asked the bartender.

The German smiled a thin smile; it wasn't a pretty sight. "You vill know zem," he said softly. "You vill most certainly know zem."

Suddenly the bartender was reminded of the quiet movements and soft fluidity of a deadly snake, and a shiver ran up his arms, making the coarse black hairs stand on end.

"Hey!" catcalled the gringo. "Come on over here and sit in my lap. I got somethin' I wanta show ya, honey." He opened his stubble-covered lips to laugh at his own humor, but the laugh never escaped the nicotine-stained barrier of his teeth.

In a single motion, so quick it was invisible to the naked eye, the German drew both his guns and fired — once, twice. The gringo slumped lifeless to the floor, his little joke to go forever unappreciated.

Behind him, three other badmen reached into their holsters, but before their guns were drawn, the German had fired again, killing them all. It was an instantaneous bloodbath — swift and merciless and, worst of all, done without malice or emotion.

"Anyvone else vit a comment?" asked the German softly, his scarred face never changing its expression.

There was only silence in the bar, silence and the acrid

smell of the dissolving gunsmoke. The German nodded ever so slightly, satisfied. He walked to the rickety swinging doors of the saloon, then turned and said quietly, "Some friends of mine vill be coming here. I hope you vill show zem more courtesy than you have shown me. Zey are not so kind-hearted as I." With those reassuring words, he was gone.

Still disbelieving — everything had happened so quickly — the *bandidos* stared for a moment at the empty doorway; then, shrugging, they went to fetch the brooms to sweep up the dead bodies. It wasn't smart to leave garbage lying around in this heat. They were merely obeying Article Four of the Badmen's Code: He might be your best friend when he's alive, but once he gets shot he's just dead meat.

The stage ride had been long, bumpy, and uncomfortable. The Three Amigos had been jammed in tightly between a fat man and his even fatter wife, who shared a loaded picnic basket filled with what smelled like raw garlic sandwiches. At the last stop before Diablo, a skinny, grizzled preacher got off the stage, but two goats and a coop full of squawking chickens got on in his place, so the coach was more crowded than before, and the goat smelled even worse than the picnic lunch. No wonder Lucky, Dusty, and Ned were a pale and lovely shade of green when they finally tumbled out of the stage into the hot and dusty main street of Diablo, right in front of the Cantina del Borrachos.

It took them a minute to straighten their backs, shake the kinks loose, and brush some of the travel stains off their fancy Amigos outfits. When they did, they looked around curiously at the godforsaken little border town, and the godforsaken little border town looked back curiously at them.

"I still don't understand the point of wearing our costumes," complained Ned. "Why don't we wear regular clothes and when we get down there change into our costumes?"

Lucky clucked his tongue impatiently. "They're expecting The Three Amigos, not three hambones in street clothes! Besides, there might be press people, there might be people who want our autographs, photographs. We don't know how big this thing is."

Ned looked around the empty streets of the border town and shook his head dubiously. So far it didn't look big at all. Then he got right to the point. "When do we get paid?"

"I'm sure after the show," said Lucky confidently.

"We should get half before and half after."

"We'll see when we get down there."

Dusty had been eyeballing the cantina during this exchange, and now he made a suggestion. "This looks like a nice place. Let's go in here."

The three pushed their way in through the swinging doors, blinking a little at the change from bright sunlight to the dim shadows of the barroom. Every head turned in their direction, and unshaven jaws dropped open in surprise. Was the circus in town?

"Looks like somebody's been down here with the ugly stick," remarked Dusty under his breath.

The three looked around them with some distaste. Not even in their bottom-of-the-barrel vaudeville days, not even in Duluth, had they seen anything as seedy as this. The sawdust on the floor hadn't been changed since President Chester A. Arthur's administration; the bar itself was splintered and pockmarked from the bullets of many guns; of the spitoon and the area around it, it was perhaps best not to speak; the mirror behind the bar was cracked and broken in several places; and even the nude lady in the painting over the mirror was one ugly broad. The clientele, though, was the worst of all. Thank God they didn't have to look them in the face. Not one of those barflies was looking an Amigo in the eye.

The focus of the desperados' attention was on the pearl-handled six-shooters hanging from Ned Nederlander's hips. The German had been wearing guns very much like these. The German. Brrrrrrr. They could hear his oily whisper even now: "Some friends of mine . . . you vill know zem . . . you vill most certainly know zem. . . . Zey are not so kind-hearted as I. . . ." These three must be zem! No matter how dumb their faces or ridiculous their outfits, these must certainly be zem . . . er, them!

As The Three Amigos headed to the bar, the badmen made a wide path for them, staying cautiously out of the way, their eyes never leaving Ned's gunbelt.

"Excuse me," said Lucky to the bartender, "we're not Mexicans. We're from out of town. Could you tell us where the big hotel is?"

"There is no big hotel here," answered the puzzled bartender.

Ned stamped his tiny foot. "Oh, great!" he pouted. "No big hotel. I could kill somebody!"

At Ned's petulant words, a ripple of fear spread through the bar, and the barflies took one giant step backward.

"Well," said Lucky, "whatever the best hotel in town is . . ."

But the bartender still shook his head. "There is no hotel in this town." Then he leaned over the bar and, with a conspiratorial wink and nod, he whispered to Lucky, "Excuse me. You are the . . ." He didn't finish the sentence: ". . . the friends of the German," but instead gave Lucky another wink.

Lucky, Dusty, and Ned blushed and grinned. They *were* the — and loved being recognized as the — Three Amigos. Who would have thought, though, that in this miserable little backwater, this pimple on the behind of Mexico, they would have fans? Just goes to show you that movies were a genuine popular miracle, a force for good, uniting all walks of life, all manner of people, all . . . er, yes. But back to the story.

"Yes, that's who we are. Pleased to meet you, we're sure. Imagine you knowing who we are. . . ."

Now the bartender leaned farther over the bar and his whisper became confidential. "I have a message for you. The German says to wait here."

"Who's the German?" Dusty asked Lucky.

"Could be the president of our fan club. Or could be the producer of the show at Santo Poco," said Lucky wisely, although he had no idea.

"Well, if we've got time to kill, I'll have a beer."

The bartender shook his head. "We have no beer. Only tequila." But he said it with respect, for the German, too, had ordered beer, and the German was nobody you'd vant to mess around vit.

"What's tequila?" Dusty wanted to know.

"It's like beer," the bartender shrugged.

"Is it fattening?" Dusty asked anxiously.

"Fattening?" What the hell was this gringo talking about? Who in God's name cared about fattening? The bartender was totally unfamiliar with the concept.

"Forget it," said Lucky. "If it's like beer, we'll have some."

"Sí" nodded the barkeep, putting a bottle of cloudy liquid and three small shot glasses on the bullet-scarred bar. "That'll be ten pesos."

"Pay the man, Ned," ordered Lucky.

Ned scowled, but obeyed. Muttering, he pulled off his boot and took out a wad of currency, all the money The Three Amigos had left in the world. In Hollywood it wasn't much, but in Diablo it counted as a fortune. Carefully pulling two bills off the wad, Ned paid for the drinks and recorded the amount under the heading "Expenses" in a little notebook he always carried. "Ten pesos, drinks, Diablo."

"Oh, come on," Dusty chuckled. "Let's have decent-size glasses."

The bartender's eyes snapped open in surprise. Larger

glasses? For *this* tequila? If it stood too long in the bottle, this tequila would eat its way right through the glass, then the varnish of the bar, and finally destroy the wood. This tequila could make a hole in water. Some *hombres*, these friends of the German!

"Sure, sure, amigos!" he cried with phony cheerfulness, and with a nervous hand he set three large tumblers next to the bottle. "Enjoy yourselves, but try not to get into too much trouble. Okay?"

Dusty picked up the bottle, and Ned the glasses. They followed Lucky to a table, which three badmen hastily vacated, knocking their chairs over in their hurry to be out of there. The others in the bar backed away as The Three Amigos approached, their eyes still fixed on Ned's pearl-handled guns.

"Boy," chuckled Lucky as he set the fallen chairs upright and sat down. "It's like these guys have never seen movie stars before."

"Give them a break." Ned was more tolerant. "People get very nervous around celebrities."

The three held their glasses up in a salute, then knocked the drinks back in one gulp. For one beat, the tops of their heads blew off and floated in the air. Then they settled back on their eyebrows.

"That's an odd taste," Ned remarked judiciously.

"Probably watered down," was Lucky's opinion.

"There's something about this place," said Ned, looking around. "Everyone is so grim."

Lucky smiled. He was feeling pretty good; in fact, pretty *damn* good. "They're just intimi . . . inmiti . . . intimidated. They've only seen us on the big screen. We're like gods to them." He gave the bar patrons an expansive grin, making certain that the celebrated Lucky Day profile was being noted and appreciated by everybody.

The *bandidos* smiled back, terrified; it was plain their hearts weren't in it.

Dusty raised another tumbler full of tequila in a mock toast. "We're just folks like you. Relax."

But Lucky had just spotted a battered old piano in a far corner of the cantina. "Dusty, go on over to the piano," he commanded.

Dusty shook his head, embarrassed, and gave his best aw-shucks grin. Even so, you could see he wasn't actually against the idea. "Been a long time. . . . I haven't played in . . ." But even as he protested, his boots were carrying him over to the old piano.

Lucky stood up and encouraged his Amigos, flinging his arms wide. "Come on, boys, let's do a little something for the folks. We're gonna do a little number for you, but remember we're a bit rusty, so bear with us."

Seated at the piano, his hands poised over the keys, Dusty smiled happily. He ran his fingers up and down the keyboard; it was out of tune, but not too badly. "Just like the old days. Ready when you are, maestro."

It *was* just like the old days, when the three of them created so much innocent joy with a happy song and a merry dance. And what better place for the recreation of that innocent joy than this broken-down cantina with its dregs of humanity? If anybody ever needed a little innocent joy, these badmen were it! Lucky walked over to the ugliest of them and, taking the *bandido's* face in his hand, he squeezed it into the semblance of a grin.

"This will bring a smile to your face."

"Now, don't join in until we tell you," cautioned little Ned with a playfully wagging finger.

"Come on, boys," laughed Lucky. "Just like we did in the old days. One . . . two . . ."

Dusty's hands began the vamp, then broke into the chorus, and Ned and Lucky began to sing and dance an old favorite, one of the highlights from their vaudeville act, good clean family fun.

Get this picture. If the badmen in the cantina had had

the smallest inkling that The Three Amigos were not the German's deadly friends, then Lucky Day, Dusty Bottoms, and Ned Nederlander would have been buzzard meat in less time than it would take to say it. It was only total, abysmal misapprehension that was keeping The Three Amigos alive, let alone prancing, mincing, and high-kicking around the sawdust to the tune of "My Little Buttercup."

But pity the poor *bandidos*. The sillier the dance got, the more terrified they became. Because if these friends of the German were stone crazy enough to get dressed to the teeth in imitation Spanish landowner outfits and sing a rotten song about moonbeams painting the sky and a cottage built for two while their hands were fluttering gaily at their hips, then they were stone crazy enough to kill every man within range of their gun barrels. After all, hadn't the German shot down three men in cold blood without turning a hair? And hadn't the German told them clearly that his friends were even worse than himself?

Nothing in the life experience of the badmen of the Borrachos cantina had prepared them for this moment. In their own way they were sheltered, knowing only simple evil — a few killings, maimings, rapings, and burnings, and a whole lot of looting. But *this* . . . this was depraved, perverse. These three gringos could sing and dance and carry on merrily while underneath they were only watching and waiting for the first opportunity to shoot the *bandidos* down like the dogs they were. How evil could men become?

So when little Ned put a napkin around his head like a babushka and became Little Buttercup, the badmen shivered and shook in their battered boots, their eyes glued to his six-guns. Who but a maniac — and a homicidal maniac at that — would dare to simper and camp and bat his eyelashes in a lowdown bar like the Cantina del Borrachos?

If these three *loco hombres* wanted to play the fool, well, there wasn't a man in the house brave enough not to go along with it. So they smiled weakly and beat time with their filthy, callused hands.

"They're loving it," whispered Lucky happily to Ned. "They're eating it up. Just look at their faces. What an audience! We should have had them in Duluth."

"Come on, everybody," called Dusty from the piano. "Sing along. *Oh, Little Buttercup, with your eyes so blue . . .*"

They sang along. Frightened and confused, they sang along. Humiliated, they sang along. Hating every single minute of it, they sang along. In a mood so murderous that *Dios* help the next *hombre* who dared to walk into the cantina, they sang along. Anything to keep those three crazy gringos from pulling those triggers.

The song came to a big finish, the finish that had wowed them in Dubuque, Peoria, and Kenosha, even though it had left them cold in Duluth. Lucky, Dusty, and Ned took their bows to puzzled applause, stole another two bows, and, flushed with success, walked out of the cantina.

Leaving behind one mixed-up bunch of desperadoes, bet on it.

"What'd I tell you?" grinned Dusty.

"Yeah, they loved us." Lucky's chuckle was complacent.

The sudden sound of a loud engine made The Three Amigos look up. A biplane was taking off from the nearby desert, flying low over their head.

"What's that?" asked Dusty.

"It's a plane," supplied Lucky helpfully.

"That's not just any plane," Ned Nederlander informed them. "It's a Tubbman 601. I flew one in *Little Neddy Goes to War.*"

"What's it doing here?" Dusty wanted to know.

"I think it's a mail plane," replied Ned.

"How can you tell?" asked Dusty, the perfect straight man.

A twinkle appeared in Ned's eye. "Didn't you notice its little balls as it flew over?" he chuckled. Then he broke up laughing, clutching his aching ribs. "Doncha get it? Mail plane, male plane . . . balls . . . oh, hee hee ha ha ha ha ha."

Lucky looked at Dusty and Dusty looked at Lucky and both of them looked at Ned but neither of them laughed because neither of them got the joke. Mail . . . male . . . little balls . . . huh?

The two Germans walked swiftly down the main street of Diablo to the Cantina del Borrachos, where word from their leader would be waiting for them. They despised this stinking little town with its dregs of humanity and its earthy smells. Most of all they despised the laziness and disorder they saw everywhere. They themselves were never lazy or untidy, even now, even here, in this oven of a hellhole. They wore fresh linen and crisp new suits and neatly fitting hats; even their shoes shone defiantly through the dust of the arid afternoon.

They pushed contemptuously past three clowns in absurd Spanish grandee costumes and overwhelmingly large sombreros and made their way into the bar, which looked and smelled even worse than they had expected.

The atmosphere in the cantina was compounded of relief at the narrow escape the *bandidos* had had with the crazies and a desire to avenge their humiliation. When the two neatly dressed men walked in, the badmen reacted like a bull at a waving flag. They charged.

"Hey, look at the two little sissies!" jeered one *bandido*.

"Yeah, ain't they purty!" another laughed roughly.

Mistake. Drawing their hidden pistols with lightning speed, the Germans fired. The two taunting badmen went down in a surprised welter of blood.

From everywhere in the cantina came the menacing click of revolvers cocking, then bullets cut through the air with deadly precision as the fire fight began. Boy, was it noisy! There was the horrid crunch of rickety tables splintering as bodies slumped onto them, the crack of railings crumbling to sawdust under the impact of wounded men, the cacophony of moans and shrieks and . . . . finally . . . silence.

Without a word, the Germans holstered their weapons and left the bar. There wasn't a scratch on them, not even a powder burn on their trigger fingers. Behind them, mayhem, a massacre. Nobody was left standing except the bartender, and *he* wasn't feeling too good himself.

Once again, a moment of pity for the poor *bandidos*. If only they'd known who the tough guys really were, they wouldn't have had to sit helplessly through a verse and three choruses of "My Little Buttercup" before they got their asses shot off.

The bartender surveyed the wreckage of his bar and the dead and dying men strewn everywhere, and he scratched his head. "This town is getting too rough for me."

Rodrigo ran eagerly into the church, where Carmen was sitting before the blank screen, her eyes closed, hands folded in prayer.

"Carmen! Carmen! The Three Amigos! I saw them in the cantina! They're here!"

"Oh, thank the Virgin!" breathed the girl. "Now we are saved!"

Chapter Seven

"But where are your horses?" asked Carmen, surprised. She had been expecting to greet The Three Amigos as she had seen them on film, mounted on swift, powerful horses who wore silver-trimmed bridles and saddles. It was startling to meet them on foot, here in the dirty streets of Diablo.

"Our horses, oh . . . yeah . . . well, you see, about the horses . . ." phumphed Lucky. The telegram hadn't said one word about horses.

"Never mind. You are here, and that's all that matters! *Gracias a Dios!*" the girl cried fervently and seized Lucky's hand, kissing it in gratitude. Then she grabbed Dusty's hand and kissed it, and looked up to see Ned already holding his out, waiting his turn. When all three hands had been thoroughly worshipped, Carmen said, "My brother Rodrigo and I, we will take you to Santo Poco."

It was a long trip, and not a comfortable one, especially for the mule, who carried Lucky, Dusty, and Ned on his back all at once. Carmen rode the burro, and Rodrigo led the way on foot, guiding the two animals by the reins wrapped around his fist.

Although The Three Amigos had filmed some of their most successful photoplays on location in Mexico, they had seen little of the country beyond the immediate settings and their portable dressing rooms. So the scenery was of interest to them, boring as it might be to others. It consisted mainly of cactus — beaver tail, saguaro, barrel, ocotillo, and cholla — interspersed between the sand and the rocks of the desert country. An occasional mesa on the horizon broke the monotony, but not by much. It wasn't the way the three movie stars were accustomed to traveling, but they made the best of it.

"Sure is pretty country around here," remarked Lucky as they rode slowly past a bleached cow skull and some rib bones, long picked clean by vultures.

"Sure is," agreed Ned, who was jammed in the middle between the other two Amigos. He averted his eyes from a scorpion making its midday meal off a tiny tickbird.

Dusty merely nodded, fascinated by a nest of rattlers coiled in the shadow of a tall, many-armed cactus. A large iguana, scaled and horned like a dragon, scuttled away between the rocks and disappeared.

"See, over the next rise, that is our village there. That is Santo Poco," Rodrigo called back in excitement.

"Not a minute too soon," complained Dusty.

"We are here," Carmen told them quietly. She slid off the burro, and The Three Amigos dismounted from the grateful mule. "We are in Santo Poco."

"Let's get rid of some of this trail dust," said Ned, beginning to slap at his clothing. Clouds of dust rose to envelop them, making them choke and cough, but by the time they had entered the village street, they were in some semblance of their old dapper selves.

The population of Santo Poco — men, women, children, chickens, goats, pigs, and flea-bitten dogs — was

ned up to greet them. This was more like it! Waving
nd grinning, The Three Amigos paraded down the street,
ooking for a reaction from their fans.

But the villagers stared back gravely, some even grimly.
Carmen and Rodrigo had been sent to bring back
efenders, heroic men of such iron that El Guapo's
andidos would flee before them. Instead, the Sanchez
hildren had returned with three gringo buffoons dressed
n silver-embroidered clown suits. No wonder they were
rim; who wouldn't be? When you need Superman, Mutt
nd Jeff just won't do.

"Whew," whispered Dusty sotto voce as he eyeballed
he wary villagers, "looks like a tough crowd."

"They probably saw *Those Darn Amigos*," Ned
peculated.

Lucky shrugged. "You're only as good as your last
icture," he sighed. This gig was going to be tougher than
hey'd thought. This was an audience that had to be won
ver. But The Three Amigos could do it, if anybody could.
hey'd have these Santo Pocanos eating out of their silver-
immed gloves. Even if they had to give them "My Little
uttercup."

"These men are The Three Amigos," Rodrigo said
roudly to farmer Pedro. "They will protect us from El
uapo."

Pedro laughed scornfully. "El Guapo will chew them
p and spit them out like flies!"

Now the little procession had reached the center of
wn, the plaza fountain, where Papa Sanchez waited
 greet them. He had prepared a solemn little speech
f thanks and had it written down on the paper he was
olding.

"Señores," he read, "welcome to Santo Poco. While
ou are with us, our home is yours. For what you are
bout to do for our village, I salute you. . . ."

But before he could get to the best part, the part about
he villain El Guapo and his murderous men, the part

where he praised The Three Amigos for risking life and limb in defense of Santo Poco against overwhelming odds. Dusty, the smartest Amigo, caught on. This head villager, mayor or something, was about to ask for an autograph.

"Here you go," he said cheerfully, taking the paper out of the old man's hands. "What's your name?"

"Papa Sanchez."

"'To Papa Sanchez,'" read Dusty as he wrote on the paper. "'Love and luck, Dusty Bottoms.'" He handed the paper back to the mystified villager. "Always glad to oblige a fan."

The solemnity of the formal moment had passed, so Sanchez merely sighed and put his little speech of welcome back into his trousers pocket. Which was probably just as well, for Lucky, Dusty, and Ned would no doubt have fainted away at its contents.

It was a very mixed group of people who gathered around the Sanchez dinner table that evening. Carmen and Rodrigo were flushed with happiness and pride having enlisted such heroes as The Three Amigos in their cause. Oh, they recognized the suspicions with which the three were regarded by the other villagers, especially their own papa, but none of the others had seen the heroes in action as had the Sanchez kids. If they had, then they'd understand. No matter how strangely they were dressed, no matter how foolishly they acted, these three were the real McCoy, or should we say the real McRodriguez?

"We are honored to have you in our home," said Mama Sanchez as she lowered a large steaming platter of tacos, refried beans, and chilies onto the center of the table.

The Sanchez table was crowded — not only the family and The Three Amigos, but also Carlos and Pedro, as representatives of the village, had been invited for dinner. And Rosita, Carmen's best friend, had begged to come. She kept her beautiful dark eyes on Dusty Bottoms, whom she regarded with passionate awe. He was so handsome

Silently she begged the Virgin to grant her Dusty's attention.

Dusty's attention, however, was on his plate and its fiery contents, which he touched tentatively and dubiously with a tin fork.

"Do you have anything besides Mexican food?"

Lucky Day swallowed a mouthful of beans, belched discreetly, and announced, "Well, I sure am looking forward to meeting this El Guapo." He grinned.

"Me, too," agreed Dusty, and Ned nodded his head.

A gasp of astonishment swept over the table. Imagine looking forward to El Guapo! These gringos had *cojones grandes*, no lie. Papa Sanchez felt suddenly ashamed. He had sadly underestimated The Three Amigos. They must truly be as heroic as his children had sworn they were. He rose to his feet.

"I want to propose a toast to some very brave men," he called out, holding high his little glass of homemade wine. "Men who would rather die than suffer injustice!"

A murmur of assent went around the table as glasses were raised.

"Who's he talking about?" Ned whispered to Lucky.

Lucky shook his head. "I don't know."

"I think it's those guys." Dusty jerked a thumb in the direction of Carlos and Pedro.

Carmen stood up. Her face was aglow, and it was lovely indeed. Her voice trembling with emotion, she took up the toast. "Men who think not of themselves but only of others. Men who would defend liberty unto death!"

"They sound incredible!" Dusty whispered to Lucky.

"Yeah," Lucky whispered back, awed. "They must be some national heroes or something."

"Men who would fight . . ." Carmen Sanchez continued, her eyes shining like twin fiery coals, "until the last drop of blood is squeezed from their bodies."

This was too much for Lucky, who was of a nature easily moved by rhetoric. Carried away, he leapt to his feet and finished the toast for Carmen. ". . . To these men!"

The villagers drew their breath in sharply. *Es verdad*, these men had the hearts of lions under those asshole outfits. To toast themselves when they were staring death right in its ugly face! What *machismo*! What true grit! Never had there been such heroes as The Three Amigos. Every villager present rose to his feet with glass raised in the toast.

"To these men!" they echoed enthusiastically, and Papa Sanchez thought, *What a pity these Three Amigos have to die like dogs.*

It was impossible for The Three Amigos to fall asleep right away; although they were exhausted and drained from the long trip and the emotion-packed supper, they were still wired on a fantastic high. Also, they hadn't slept three in a bed since Duluth.

Ned Nederlander, Lucky Day, and Dusty Bottoms lay quietly in the moonlight, in the old carved bed in which Mama and Papa Sanchez had slept for thirty years but which had been lent to the heroic Amigos out of Sanchez gratitude. Mellow September moonlight streamed in through the bedroom window, and the night breezes wafted the soft, sweet scent of the bougainvillea to their happily tuckered-out nostrils.

"What a nice family," said Ned quietly.

"They really are," agreed Lucky.

"That Mama Sanchez is really a wonderful cook."

"How's this show supposed to work, anyway?" asked Dusty. He'd had the question on his mind all evening.

"Well, I talked to Rodrigo tonight. He's the kid," Lucky replied. "He's a little hazy on the details, but as far as I can figure, El Guapo is coming in a day or two. He rides in and acts like he owns the place. He'll have about forty or fifty other actors with him. We come out, put on a big show, run him off . . ."

"Hmmmm," mused Ned. "Sounds like a big production. And then what?"

Lucky thought about it for a few seconds. "Well," he said at last, "I guess we're supposed to do pretty much what we did in *Shootin' For Love.*"

Ned Nederlander smiled nostalgically into the moonlight. "That was a good movie," he whispered fondly.

"They all were, Ned," whispered Lucky back.

"Yeah, they sure were." Ned closed his eyes, a sweet, babyish smile on his small face.

For a minute or two there was silence in the room, then Lucky whispered softly, "Dusty?"

"Yeah?"

"Dusty, what are you gonna do with your share of the money?"

Dusty Bottoms didn't have to think about it. "A car, Lucky," he answered promptly. "A big, shiny silver car. I'm gonna drive it all over Hollywood, show Flugleman a thing or two. What about you?"

"What about me?" laughed Lucky and then his voice grew dreamy. "I've always wanted to travel. New York, maybe Paris . . . drink a lot of champagne, go to a lot of important parties, be a big shot. . . . How about you, Ned?"

"I'm gonna start a fund to help homeless children," said Ned.

"Oh, that occurred to me at one point, too," Dusty put in hastily. "I'll do that first and *then* get a shiny new car."

"Right, right," Lucky chimed in. "Any money left over from the homeless children would go into travel. Travel is important, but homeless children are important, too. . . ."

"Sure," Dusty agreed. "Homeless children are good. I mean, put your money into that and you know you're doing something."

"That's what I always say," echoed Lucky.

One by one, their voices died away. One by one, their weary eyelids shut, first Ned's, then Dusty's, and finally, Lucky's. The sandman came and bonked them on the heads with his heavy sack of sand. Soon they were all asleep, and the gentle night silence was broken only by the sound of their snoring.

Good thing, too. Tomorrow would be a busy day, even busier than The Three Amigos expected. Much busier.

The ringing of the village church bells woke the people of Santo Poco every morning at daybreak, and this morning was no different from the others. The clanging startled The Three Amigos awake, and they tumbled out of bed.

For a moment they were disoriented, not quite certain where they were or what they were supposed to be doing here, but recollection soon returned. They were here to put on a show. A one-day appearance in full costume, which would net the trio a hundred thousand bucks . . . no, pesos, but what the hell? Money was money, right?

The entire village was waking up — roosters crowing, babies bawling, dogs running into the town square to scratch their fleas in public. Already the first of the farmers were heading off to the cornfields, their machetes on their shoulders, to continue with the harvest. It was time for The Three Amigos to be up and doing. Getting into those costumes took time if they were to look good, and then there was the matter of breakfast. . . .

Manuel, Rafael Jesús, and Perrito were feeling no pain. Among them they had finished a bottle and a half of rotgut tequila in under two hours; now they were three sheets to the wind and ready for some action. The tequila had brought out the belligerence and nastiness of their *bandido* natures; one or two drinks and they were looking to kick ass. Now they'd had five or six apiece and were ready for another world war.

Manuel held up the empty liquor bottle and regarded it with a heavy scowl. Then he hurled it viciously against a rock and watched it smash into a thousand bright shards of splintered glass.

"Let us go get some more tequila."

Perrito looked around nervously. "El Guapo said to wait here," he reminded them.

"Awww, by the time he gets here, we'll be back," shrugged Rafael Jesús.

Perrito considered this for a moment, then he, too, shrugged. True, El Guapo had posted them here as pickets because he intended to ride against the village of Santo Poco tomorrow, and he wanted to make certain that the coast was kept clear. But the need for another bottle of booze struck him as urgent, and obtaining it a top priority. Besides, what could possibly happen? Were they not practically in the middle of the desert, where the *federales* never dared to track them? Who could sneak up on El Guapo across terrain like this, even without a guard on watch? No, it was safe to leave their posts as long as El Guapo never found out. If he did, he'd whip their asses for sure.

In a moment, all three were in the saddle, swaying a little from the effects of the tequila.

"We will go down to Santo Poco," announced Manuel, showing broken, stained, and missing teeth in a wolfish grin. "They will be glad to see us."

Pulling their guns from their holsters, the laughing bandits fired a few shots in the air to get the party rolling. Then, urging their horses on with cruel slashes of their shining spurs, they rode hell for leather toward the God-fearing little farming village.

"I still think they should give us part of the money now," grumbled Ned, wriggling into his tight Amigo trousers.

"Ned," Dusty explained firmly. "This is a town. Towns

do not run away. We'll get the money. Let's hear your speech."

Pouting, Ned turned away. "I know my speech," he retorted defensively.

"Do it, then," ordered Lucky.

"All right, all right! Sheeesh! 'Wherever there is injustice,'" began Ned Nederlander at top speed and without emphasis or punctuation, " 'you will find us wherever there is suffering we'll be there ... blah blah blah....' Then El Guapo says, 'You will die like dogs,' and Dusty says ..."

" 'We will not die like dogs, we will fight like lions,'" put in Dusty, who was very proud of this line.

"Great, great!" Lucky applauded. "Now that's what you should be worrying about, not the money. We'll get the money." He turned back approvingly to his reflection in the small mirror over the bureau, but was soon jostled out of the way by Dusty and Ned demanding equal time with the looking glass. Blissfully unaware of the drunken and bloodthirsty *bandidos* riding swiftly toward Santo Poco, The Three Amigos continued to take their time dressing. They were actors now, no longer common, ordinary men, actors with a show to do, and they weren't going to stint the natives on any single detail.

Below their window, the little village square was a hive of activity. The mill wheel was grinding, turning slowly in its endless, creaking circle, dragged by the patient oxen. The sewing machines were humming busily, and at the well in the center of the village, young women had gathered to draw water for their households and to exchange tidbits of gossip.

"Which one of The Three Amigos do you like the best, Carmen?" Rosita's dark eyes sparkled with mischief.

Carmen's lovely face grew dreamy. "I like the one who is not so smart," she confessed with a blush.

Rosita's feathery dark brows drew together in a frown

of puzzlement. "Which one is that?" she asked in understandable confusion. Yes, which one *was* that?

But Carmen had been caught off guard, or she would never had allowed herself to make so immodest an admission. Now she tossed her head impatiently, and a few drops of water spilled from her *olla*. "Rosita, how can you ask such a question when these men are about to risk their lives tomorrow?"

The sound of pounding hooves rapidly approaching made the girls break off, startled and suddenly afraid.

"Madre de Dios!" cried Juanita. *"Bandidos! Bandidos!"*

"Sooner than expected," muttered Carmen, dropping her water bucket. "I must warn The Three Amigos!"

Like a herd of deer surprised by hunters, the girls scattered, running toward the houses to warn the village.

At the sound of the alarm, the village swung into action — locking doors and barring shutters, emptying the streets of children, goats, pigs, chickens, and even cats and dogs.

"They are coming! They are coming!" Carmen yelled up to the room shared by The Three Amigos.

Lucky poked his head out of the window. "Who?"

"El Guapo and his men!" cried Carmen, her huge eyes luminous with fear.

Lucky gave a little start of surprise. "Already? We'll begin to get ready, then." He pulled his head in and turned to his amigos. "Jeez, I think we've got to do the show now," he announced.

"Oh, great! I thought we were gonna get a rehearsal!" Dusty sounded pretty annoyed.

But Lucky Day only shrugged. "So what? They've probably done it a million times, and we know what *we're* doing."

"So what," retorted Dusty, pissed off. "It's going to take me at least a half hour to get ready." He turned back to the mirror, fidgeting with his pleated bow tie, which would *not* lie straight beneath his collar. Also, the ruffles on his shirt were mussed.

"We haven't got that long," snapped Lucky. "Ned, you sure of your lines?"

"I know 'em, I know 'em," grumbled Ned, who prided himself on being a professional.

Dusty seemed to be slowing down deliberately out of pique. With agonizing slowness, he put the finishing touches to his outfit while Ned and Lucky looked on in frustration, grinding their teeth. Now Dusty was polishing each and every silver concho on his belt one by one.

They could hear the riders entering the village, their horses' unshod hooves making a thumping sound on the street of packed earth. Lucky went back to the window to see if he could get a glimpse of them; after all, they were all going to have to do a show together within the next half hour, and he wanted to be sure that El Guapo didn't outshine The Three Amigos in the costume department. "Looks like there are about three of them," he announced.

"Perfect," Ned sniffed sarcastically. "Rodrigo said there would be fifty, and now there are three. They'd better not try to cut our money."

"Dusty!" Lucky called impatiently. "Are you ready?"

"No." Dusty was buckling on his belt very slowly and carefully.

Meanwhile, El Guapo's men had reached the center of town. They pulled sharply on their horses' reins, forcing the animals to rear up, their hooves cutting the air, while the *bandidos* fired bullets at the cactus and spider plants, at the jars of water cooling under the overhangs of the roofs, and even took some random potshots at the scurrying dogs.

"Tequila!" roared Manuel. "Are you going to bring us some tequila or do we have to come in and get it ourselves? You would not like that, we promise you!"

Locked inside their adobe houses, the villagers remained silent and invisible.

"Hey, these guys are pretty good," approved Lucky. The Three Amigos were peeking out of their bedroom window to see how their co-stars were shaping up.

"Are you kidding?" sniffed Ned snobbishly. "They're doing every cliché in the book." They were also a lot grubbier than Ned had imagined, filthy and unshaved. That was off-putting to anybody as fastidious as Ned. Where was their pride? Where was their showmanship?

Lucky smoothed the lapels of his precious Amigos jacket. "Let's give 'em about thirty more seconds."

"If I have to go into the cantina, someone is going to die!" Manuel threatened at the top of his lungs.

As though that were the cue speech, Lucky turned to the other two. "Okay, Amigos, we're on. Ned, big smile. Dusty, just relax and have fun with it." There was a little flurry of last-minute activity as the Amigos smoothed back their hair and readjusted those huge sombreros, brushed imaginary specks of dust off their costumes, and — in the case of Dusty — anxiously checked the conchos on the gunbelt to make certain they were dazzling.

"Where's our tequila? We're waiting!" yelled Rafael Jesús, his guns drawn menacingly. Above his head, he could hear somebody counting in English: "One, two, three . . . NOW!" Before the *bandidos* knew what was coming off, three gringos in full costume had somersaulted off the low balcony of one of the adobe houses and were standing side by side, grinning up at them.

"I'm Lucky Day," cried the one with the white hair and the profile.

"I'm Ned Nederlander," piped the littlest one.

"I'm Dusty Bottoms," declared the tallest one. Then they all three spoke in chorus: "And together we're The Three Amigos!"

As the astonished badmen sat speechless and disbelieving in the saddle, staring at *Dios*-knows-what, the three costumed men, with a dramatic flourish, performed the famous Three Amigos salute — one, two: hands crossed on chest; three: hands on hips. Before any one of the *bandidos* could recover and make a move, The Three Amigos danced lightly to the center of the square and vaulted onto the backs of the horses provided for them by the villagers.

All over Santo Poco, shutters were pushed open an inch — just an inch — and terrified yet curious faces were pressed to the windows. Upstairs in the Sanchez home, Carmen, who was more courageous than most of the men, pushed her window entirely open to get a better view. After all, these three were *her* heroes, and how they conducted themselves with these villainous murderers was of first consequence to her.

Now The Three Amigos, mounted, rode their horses confidently up to the *bandidos* and did a little show, a few threatening grimaces and defiant gesticulations, one or two rearings of the horses, just the ordinary theatrical preliminaries that whet an audience's appetite for action.

El Guapo's men could do nothing but stare. They had never seen anything like The Three Amigos in all their lives.

Lucky, Dusty, and Ned stared back, waiting for El Guapo's actors to speak the first line.

Silence. Stunned silence. Nothing but incredulous silence as the tipsy bandits tried to figure out who and what the hell these gringos were. They hadn't been asking for much, right? All they'd come for was one little bottle of tequila; instead, they appeared to have become trapped in an insane asylum's annual masquerade party.

Lucky shrugged. It looked as though it was up to the Amigos. He broke rank and rode out alone for the confrontation until he was eyeball to eyeball with Manuel. Lowering his voice to its deepest register, he began.

"Well, you dirt-eating pieces of slime. You scum-sucking pigs. You sons of a motherless goat . . ." It was a good opening, a standard gambit of defiance. Lucky was quite pleased with it, actually, and he glanced back at his fellow Amigos with a little wink of self-congratulation.

"Son of a motherless goat?" repeated Manuel slowly. "And who are you?"

This was Ned's cue. Kneeing his horse forward until it was abreast of Lucky's, he recited, "Wherever there is injustice you will find us. Wherever there is suffering we'll be there. . . . Uh, shit." He'd forgotten what came next. "Line!" he called impatiently.

Dusty rode up next to him. "Wherever liberty is threatened, you will find . . ."

"Okay, I got it now," said Ned. "Wherever liberty is threatened you will find . . ."

"THE THREE AMIGOS!" they all finished at once at the top of their lungs.

Papa Sanchez joined Carmen at the window, his hand clutching at his daughter's shoulder. So much was at stake here. If these men should fail . . . His fingers tightened, and Carmen winced. They must not fail.

Now The Three Amigos had drawn their guns and were riding in circles around the *bandidos*, firing blanks, determined to give their audience its money's worth. *"Arriba!"* they cried. *"Arriba! Arriba!"*

El Guapo's men, completely dumbfounded, could only sit and stare, their tobacco-stained mouths agape.

"Who are these monkeys?" Perrito asked Manuel.

"I don't know."

"Should we kill them?" inquired Rafael Jesús.

Manuel thought hard about it for a minute. Even through the fog of tequila he could perceive that this was no ordinary set of circumstances. This was something new, something perhaps of use to their leader. "No," he decided. "Let's go tell El Guapo what we have seen here."

They jerked on their reins, turning the horses around, then the three badmen rode out of town without firing a shot.

So that was that. Frankly, it was not quite what The Three Amigos had envisioned back in Hollywood. They had pictured a large stadium, masses of people waving little flags, vendors of tacos and chilies and refried beans, and events including fancy riding, roping, and shooting, a kind of Buffalo Bill Cody show with Mexican seasoning. What had become of the big production? Also, they were very disappointed in the El Guapo side of the contingent. Where was the flash? Where was the dash? Where were the costumes? Where were the rest of the actors? Still, it was not a production of The Three Amigos. *They* had done *their* part; nobody could blame *them*.

"Nice show," Lucky complimented them.

"Not bad for a matinee," agreed Dusty.

But little Ned's face was clouded. "Damn it! I forgot my line!"

"Hey, forget it," Lucky told him, giving Ned's shoulder a pat.

"Yeah, I don't even think they noticed," said Dusty.

"Think so?" Ned's eyes brightened a little.

"Positive," the others assured him.

The doors and windows of Santo Poco opened slowly as the astounded villagers began to emerge from their hiding places. It hardly seemed possible, although they had witnessed it with their own eyes. These three outrageously dressed gringos had actually sent El Guapo's men packing, riding off in fear of their lives! Who would have believed it! For the first time, the people of Santo Poco looked at Ned Nederlander, Lucky Day, and Dusty Bottoms with new eyes, eyes filled with respect and, yes, even awe.

Carmen ran out of the house and across the square. She was so filled with pride she could have kissed them all, for hadn't it been she who had brought them here and had championed them when the others had made fun of their outfits? Yes. Now they had done her proud.

"*Viva* Amigos," said Papa Sanchez quietly, and Rodrigo

picked up the cheer. "*Viva* Amigos!!" cried the boy. Now the entire village took up the chant. "*Viva Amigos!!* VIVA AMIGOS!!!"

"They're really starved for entertainment around here," Lucky smiled indulgently.

"I'm telling you, I've been in this situation before," said Ned urgently, tugging at Lucky's sleeve. "Ask for the money now while they're still excited."

"You were magnificent!" cried Carmen as she reached them. Her eyes were glowing and her face was flushed; a tinge of deep rose in her cheeks matched the soft color of her lips.

"We were okay," said Lucky offhandedly, playing it cool.

The bells in the church tower began to peal out a clanging song of victory. The merry sound infected the villagers with relief and happiness. It could have been a slaughter, a massacre, but instead these three heroes had been *macho* enough to terrorize the bandits without a drop of blood being shed. What this called for was a celebration.

"Fiesta!" cried one villager.

"Fiesta!" cried another.

"Fiesta! Fiesta! Fiesta!"

Chapter Eight

While the happy residents of Santo Poco were digging the pit and setting up the spits for the pork barbecue, while the mariachi band was tuning up and the prettiest girls in the village were heating up the irons to press out the ruffles in their party dresses, Manuel, Rafael Jesús, and Perrito were stammering out the day's unbelievable events to El Guapo in his mountain fastness. Although the bandit leader did not actually appear to be paying any attention, he was actually taking in every word.

In the year 1645 a Jesuit priest named Father Francesco Aguerra had journeyed from Spain to the mountains of Mexico to build a mission for the order. Although he had taken a vow of poverty, Father Francesco had grown up as the second son of one of the wealthiest families in Andalusia, and his idea of poverty had to be seen to be believed. The mission, when completed, was a castle, complete with a drawbridge and a moat. High ceilings, vast rooms, formal gardens, a huge central courtyard, tiled roofs, fireplaces large enough to roast entire oxen, a separate chapel the size of a cathedral — all of these would have made Mission Escorial a showplace back in the Old Country. But here in Mexico, who was to see it, apart from a mountain lion or two and an army of scorpions?

For 250 years the palatial mission languished, while the number of priests and monks who inhabited it grew smaller from decade to decade. At last, when the twentieth century was but eleven years old, there were only two holy brothers left; one of them was blind and the other used to hear saintly voices telling him to save New Jersey. It was then that El Guapo the *bandido* found Mission Escorial.

Because he wasn't all bad all the way through, El Guapo didn't actually kill the two friars. He allowed them to stay on when he took possession of the mission with his ragtag band of *bandidos*. Brother Juniper, the blind one, could sweep a little and make the beds, even though he kept bumping into the bureaus. Brother Diego, the crazy one, was a mean hand with the tortillas and ended his days mixing *masa* and stirring *salsa* in the mission kitchen. Out of the goodness of his heart, El Guapo didn't overcharge them on the rent, either. But those two had been dead for several years now, and the abandoned mission was now El Guapo's totally.

It was his castle, and he was king of it. It pleased him to be the lord of so many large, fine rooms, and the owner of so many vivid paintings of the Crucifixion and holy statues dripping blood from their wounds. He was not an irreligious man, and living in a mission had brought El Guapo nearer to God, or so he thought. It put a kind of imprimatur on his dastardly acts.

Of course, it was no longer a mission, despite the religious artifacts which were still hanging around wherever one looked. It was a bandit stronghold, easy to defend, impossible to capture. El Guapo had set up watchtowers at the corners of the walls, and these were always manned by his sharpest-eyed men. Its position in the mountains gave the mission a wide overview of the surrounding terrain. Nothing and nobody could approach without being seen. Moreover, it now housed an army of men, far more badmen than El Guapo ever took with him on any raid, rapine, or robbery. Nobody but El Guapo himself knew exactly how many *bandidos* were under his command, because El Guapo had no intention of revealing his strength to any of his enemies. And he had many of those, from the Mexican Federal troops — *los federales* — to every farmer and villager within raiding radius.

It took a great deal of grain to feed an army, especially an army of badmen, who are notoriously big eaters. El Guapo had to spend an even larger proportion of his time raiding villages like Santo Poco to keep on top of the food situation.

But not all his time. El Guapo had hobbies. Next to arson, rape, pillage, and mayhem, El Guapo loved photography best.

The art of photography was about 75 years old in 1916, and El Guapo was one of its passionate devotees. He was the proud owner of a state-of-the-art Bell camera and developing equipment, and he liked nothing better than to create elaborate tableaux in full costume for himself to photograph. He would send these photographs in to the glossy magazines, hoping for publication, but the magazines kept sending them back.

Just now, as his three *bandidos* blurted out their story of the lunatic gringos in Santo Poco, El Guapo was still setting up his latest fantasy. His head was buried under the black cloth behind the camera, and he was peering at the arrangement of half-clad women which appeared upside down in his lens.

It was supposed to be a Turkish seraglio, the harem of a sultan. A selection of the plumpest of his women had been dressed in what El Guapo believed to be the eastern style, complete with beads and spangles and bare midriffs, and were posed appetizingly in terrified positions. They were intended to appear oh-so-frightened of their lord and master, who brandished a large scimitar over their lovely heads. Jefe had been drafted to play the Sultan, dressed in flowing pantaloons and topped with turban (El Guapo spared no expense for the props).

El Guapo clicked his tongue in irritation. The pose was close to being right, but not yet perfect. Scowling, he pulled his head out from under the cloth.

"And then what happened?" he demanded.

"They got on their horses," answered Manuel, "and rode around firing their *pistoles* in the air."

"Jefe!" barked the bandit leader. "The sword! Hold the sword higher! Remember you are a sultan!"

"The sword is so heavy, El Guapo," whined his second in command. "How long do I have to stand like this?"

"Until I am satisfied!"

"And they called us scum-sucking pigs," put in Rafael Jesús indignantly. "Us!"

"More frightened, girls!" called El Guapo. "Like this, see?" He pantomimed terror, and the women copied him, widening their eyes and putting their hands to their brows.

"What should we do, El Guapo?" asked Perrito.

El Guapo made a minute adjustment in the camera. "Tomorrow I will take fifty men with me, find these three gringos, open their stomachs, grab their intestines, and squeeze the *shit* out of them!" Once again he ducked under the camera hood. "Hold it! That's perfect!"

The flash powder exploded, and one more masterpiece was captured on film. El Guapo smiled; he was very happy.

The village of Santo Poco was very happy, too. It was party time; fiesta was in full swing. There was homemade wine and home-brewed beer for everybody, even a small sip apiece for the *niños*, the littlest kids. The music of guitars, mandolins, and mariachis filled the night air. There were fireworks — rockets, sparklers, and catherine wheels. And everywhere the people were dancing, the men in their best striped serapes, the girls and women in their prettiest dresses. And The Three Amigos were the heroes of the hour. Had they not saved Santo Poco?

Lucky was dancing with Carmen, who swayed in his arms as lightly as a beautiful feather. Carmen wore a flower in her hair, and its aroma was almost as intoxicating to Lucky Day as the wine he had drunk, the applause he'd been given, and his own wonderfulness.

"Lucky, tell me what it is like where you are from," whispered the girl.

"I come from a place called Hollywood," he began.

"Yes, that is where I sent the telegram. Is it beautiful?"

"Oh, very beautiful. It's just a little town, kind of a crossroads. But there are orange groves everywhere and the air smells wonderful and you can see the mountains in the distance covered with snow. . . ." Lucky's voice grew husky as he thought of home.

"Do you think it will ever change?" asked Carmen softly.

The music stopped, but the two of them continued to dance, pressed closely together. "Oh, no," replied Lucky. "Santo Poco will probably be a big bustling town one day. But I think Hollywood will always be the same."

"You know so much, Lucky," breathed the girl.

"Well, I do have an intuition about these things . . . that's why I'm the leader." He turned his face away, ever so subtly, so that Carmen Sanchez could get a good look at his profile and be suitably impressed. Which, of course, she was.

While Carmen was dancing with Lucky, Rosita had moved in on the man of her dreams, Dusty Bottoms. She found him noodling on a Spanish guitar, strumming softly, masterfully evoking the sound of a cat being slowly and painfully strangled. He was vocally accompanying those sounds by an off-key rendering of something that resembled flamenco as closely as Minnie Mouse resembles Christie Brinkley.

Rosita sat down close to Dusty and watched him play for a while. She was so enchanted by him that even his singing didn't turn her off.

"Do you have a girlfriend back home, Dusty? she asked at last.

"Me? Oh, no. Never really had time for that sort of thing, being so busy." Had it not been dark out, Rosita might have perceived his blushes.

"Have you ever kissed a girl?"

"Oh, sure. Lots. Lots of times," Dusty lied.

"Would you like to kiss me?" she asked him softly.

"Um, yeah. . . ." said Dusty, and bent his attention back to his guitar.

"Well . . .?"

"What, now?" Dusty looked up nervously. Rosita was evidently waiting, for her luscious lips were pursed in an unmistakable invitation.

"Well," laughed the girl, "we could take a walk and you could kiss me on the veranda. . . ."

"The lips will be fine," Dusty assured her hastily.

Just as Lucky and Dusty had captured the attention of maidens, so Ned, too, had found his audience. He was having the time of his life explaining to the children of Santo Poco exactly what it means to be an actor, how to take hold of an emotion and make it work for you, how to find your motivation in any scene, how to *become* the person you're portraying. The children sat fascinated, their chins on their fists, watching him closely. It wasn't that they understood a word he was saying, or cared about any of it. They were waiting for him to do some tricks with those pearl-handled revolvers of his.

"One time," Ned went on, aware of his audience's total attention, "Dorothy Gish was visiting me on the set of *Little Neddy Grab Your Guns*, and she said to me . . . she said, 'Ned, you have it. Whatever an actor needs, you have it.' And another time D.W. told me . . . C.B. once said to me . . . But to play an emotion, you must first center it. And then you let it come. And when your emotions connect with the audience . . ." Ned put his hand over his heart. "There's no feeling like it. And yet, I think that what I want ultimately is to direct. Because the director has the complete control. . . . His is the power to . . ."

The children sighed inwardly, wondering whether this gringo was ever going to shut his mouth and open his holsters. They were getting calluses on their butts just sitting here waiting.

All in all, though, it was a hell of a party, and it was three very tired and very happy Amigos who tumbled into their single bed. The hour was well past midnight, and they were a little drunk, so sleep came immediately and soundly. Good night, Amigos. You've done a good day's work and you deserve your rest.

This time the church bells didn't stop their clangor. They went on ringing, ringing, ringing . . . and there was a note of terror in the peals.

"Next time we come here I'm going to ask for a different room," grumbled Dusty, only half awake. His head was throbbing painfully and last night some nasty little gremlins had held a poker game in his mouth. At least that's what it tasted like.

There was a loud knocking at the door, and Carmen burst in, breathless with excitement.

"Amigos! El Guapo himself is here . . . with all his men! Just outside the village! I have your horses waiting; you must ride against him now!" She ran out, her eyes shining. Once more her heroes would get a chance to prove their valor, especially Lucky.

Ned sat up in bed. "What is she talking about?"

"I don't know," shrugged Lucky. He got out of bed slowly so that his hangover wouldn't be jarred, and walked to the window to see what he could.

Men were strung out across the far horizon just at

the edge of the village. Mounted men, armed men. There were at least thirty or forty of them, perhaps more.

"Looks like we've got another show to do," reported Lucky.

"Great," muttered Dusty sarcastically. The gremlins in his mouth had emptied their ashtrays onto his tongue, and they'd all been smoking nickel cigars.

"Let's get it over with," said Ned, hopping out of bed in his nightshirt and reaching for his pants.

They dressed quickly, without yesterday's attention to detail and without jockeying for position at the mirror. Dusty didn't even bother to polish his conchos. They were conscious that the day before had been only a curtain raiser and this must be the main event, but they couldn't quite recapture all that famous Three Amigos pep and enthusiasm, thanks to the partying they had done last night. Still, the show must go on and they could surely fake it; besides, they hadn't been paid yet.

"Let's go," said their leader, Lucky, when they were ready.

They left the Sanchez *casa*. This time the natives of Santo Poco were waiting outside their houses to watch them ride. No more locked doors; no more barred windows and closed shutters. They now had complete faith in their heroes.

"They are so brave," whispered Rosita, clutching Carmen's arm.

"May the Virgin protect them," Carmen whispered back. "Let them not die."

The Three Amigos mounted their horses and rode slowly out to meet El Guapo. Just as slowly, the bandit chieftain rode forward to meet The Three Amigos. In the center of the village square, both factions came to a halt. They were almost face to face.

Geez, thought Lucky. This El Guapo is some serious ugly!

How ugly was he?

Why, man, he was so ugly that when he was born, his father didn't pass out cigars, he passed out barf bags!

"It's a pleasure working with you," Lucky said as a showman-to-showman courtesy. But he said it under his breath, so that the villagers wouldn't hear. Out loud, what he said was "Well, you dirt-eating piece of slime. You scum-sucking pig. You son of a motherless goat."

Incredibly, Manuel and the others hadn't lied. There *were* three lunatic gringos dressed in monkey suits here in Santo Poco, and they were just as crazy as the guards had reported.

"Who are you? demanded El Guapo.

Ned rode up. "Wherever there is injustice you will find us; wherever there is suffering we'll be there." He leaned forward in his saddle and whispered to El Guapo. "Tell us we will die like dogs."

"What?" The Bandit chief's eyebrows disappeared into his filthy sombrero.

"Tell us we will die like dogs," prompted Ned urgently.

El Guapo looked over at Jefe. They shrugged, mystified.

"You will die like dogs!" declared El Guapo obligingly.

"No!" cried Dusty with passion. "We will not die like dogs. We will fight like lions, because we are . . ."

"THE THREE AMIGOS!" they roared in chorus, then executed the famous Three Amigos salute — one, two: hands crossed on chest; three; hands on hips. Drawing their guns, they began to circle the bandits on their horses, shooting their six-guns into the air and showing off with little pieces of fancy stunt riding. Lucky even pulled out his lariat and demonstrated some of his special tricks with a rope.

"*Arriba!*" they shouted. "*Arriba!! Arriba!!!*" And they fired off their blanks. So far so good; it seemed to be going quite well. The villagers were certainly watching them pop-eyed with admiration.

El Guapo sat amazed; it was exactly as his men had described it. But what the hell was it? His curiosity was piqued.

"I like these guys," he said to Jefe. "These are funny guys. Just kill one of them."

The bandit nodded. He cocked his rifle and sighted it over his left arm, taking careful aim. He fired once. Lucky Day pitched out of his saddle and fell to the ground. Carmen Sanchez uttered a short, high-pitched scream.

"Hold it!" yelled Dusty. "Just hold it!" He and Ned rode over to their fallen Amigo and dismounted. Lucky was just managing to sit up, still dazed. He was clutching his arm, and the arm was bleeding.

"Jeez, Lucky, you all right?" asked Dusty worriedly.

"What happened?" demanded Ned.

Lucky's face contorted in pain. "I don't know." He looked at his arm, and his eyes widened. "Oooh, my arm! Look! Blood!" Whirling to confront the bandit, Lucky found Jefe's rifle still pointed at him. This was definitely wrong. This was not in the script. This was not the way they were supposed to be playing it. Lucky scowled and marched over to the bandit second in command, holding out his hand.

"Wait a second! C'mon, c'mon, gimme that!" Snatching the Enfield out of the astounded Jefe's hands, he broke the cartridge chamber open and spilled the bullets out into his palm.

"Oh great! Real bullets! I'll just keep these for proof!" To El Guapo, Lucky hissed, "You're in a lot of trouble, mister!"

This was the moment when Lucky Day learned the truth.

Now, for the first time, Lucky locked gazes with the bandits, and what he read there made his blood run cold. With a question in his eyes, he turned his face from one to the other, from the villainous Jefe to the murderous El Guapo, who sat smiling coldly back, the evil in the smile telling Lucky more than he wanted to know. All at once the entire scenario was clear. And, oh, was it ever a worst-case scenario! The words of the telegram came back to him; only this time he could read a very different meaning into them. They were in trouble, bad trouble. The three of them were up shit creek, and some dummy had lost the paddle.

There was no mistaking those faces and those cold, murderous smiles. These were no players; these dudes were the genuine article — real heavy-duty badasses. They were all gonna die!

"Oh, excuse me," said Lucky, patting El Guapo nervously on the arm. He turned and walked back to the other Amigos, a frozen smile painted on his face.

"It's real," he said to Dusty and Ned through clenched teeth.

"What?" No comprehension.

"It's real! This is real!"

"You mean . . ." stammered the horrified Ned as light began to dawn.

"Yes," nodded Lucky. "They're going to kill us."

El Guapo the horrible and his desperadoes pay Santo Poco an unfriendly visit.

You're only as good as your last picture—Flugleman fires The Three Amigos.

Not such a lucky day for Lucky Day—wardrobe takes back the suit.

ABOVE: Some days you can't make a living in a town like Diablo.

RIGHT: The beautiful Carmen Sanchez and her brother Rodrigo greet The Three Amigos, Santo Poco's saviors.

Even a bandit needs a hobby.

We ride! We fight! We love! Martin Short as Ned Nederlander, Chevy Chase as Dusty Bottoms, and Steve Martin as Lucky Day, "and together we're ... THE THREE AMIGOS!"

El Guapo withdraws his "protection" from Santo Poco, and Jefe blows up the church.

"Viva El Guapo!" Jefe and the bandits celebrate their leader's birthday.

The birthday boy cutting a mean rug.

"Happy birthday to our favorite 33-year-old." Jefe, El Guapo, the German—but where's the cake?

Lucky tries to crash the party without an invitation.

"So I should just wait here, then?"

"And we plundered . . . and . . . pruned . . . the hedges . . ."

Ned can draw and shoot like a demon; now if only he could lift the gun . . .

Dusty fights off El Guapo alone; Lucky and Ned just hang around.

Those are real bullets they're shooting. The Three Amigos become true heroes at last.

Chapter Nine

"Yes," nodded Lucky. "They're going to kill us."

It took a moment or two for his words to sink in, but when they did, and when the enormity of their situation imprinted itself on their consciousness, the same words flashed through the brains of Ned and Dusty at the same instant.

We're all gonna die!

I don't want to die, I'm too young, thought Dusty, and his handsome face crumpled. Tears gushed out of his eyes and down his round cheeks, and his nose began to run.

I don't want to die, I'm much too young, thought Ned, and he too burst into tears. "What . . . what am I doing in Mexico?" he sobbed.

"I've been shot already!" wailed Lucky, and big salty tears welled up under his eyelids.

"I know!" Ned wailed back.

"What are we going to do?" wept Dusty.

"Well, we're not going to get paid; that's for sure," sniffled Ned, and the thought of it made The Three Amigos cry even harder.

But they couldn't go on crying forever. There had to be a way out. You don't just kill off three movie stars like *that*! Fame and popularity had to count for something, right? Even if their last picture was a bomb, even if Flugleman had thrown them out on their keesters, even if their fans had torn up their autographs, you don't go *kill* somebody for that!

"Let me talk to him man to man," cried Lucky, as the natual leader.

Wiping at his eyes with the ruffled cuff of his shirt, he walked slowly over to the mounted bandits, Dusty and Ned trailing in his wake.

Lucky took off his sombrero and gazed humbly and earnestly up at the bandit chief. "Mr. Guapo, I'd just like to say on behalf of The Three Amigos that we're very sorry, and we're going to go home now. See, there's been a big misunderstanding."

A huge gasp arose from the aghast villagers as they watched in horror the sight of their heroes evaporating into thin air.

"See," put in Dusty helpfully, "we're not gunmen. We're movie stars."

"Movie stars?" El Guapo's cigarillo pointed straight up like a question mark.

"Yes," Ned smiled boyishly. "Actors. Entertainers. We sing and we dance."

"Yeah," Lucky added. "You know ... one, two ..."

And without preamble they broke into the first verse of "My Little Buttercup," giving it everything they had. Never had they kicked so high or camped so low; this was a matter of life and death. Three precious behinds depended on this audition.

A low moan escaped the villagers, who now realized

for the first time that they had made one huge mistake. Performers! Actors! *Cobardes*, that's what they were. Silly cowards with not one single *cojone* among them!

The song came to an end, trailing off into an uncomfortable silence, while The Three Amigos waited nevously for El Guapo's verdict.

The *bandido's* ugly face broke into an evil, blood-chilling smile, his specialty. "Don't you want to die like dogs?" he asked maliciously.

"If there's any way of avoiding that part of it, we'd be very, very much in your debt," answered Dusty with enormous sincerity.

The bandit leader uttered a snort of contempt, then he took the cigarillo from his mouth and spat deliberately at the dirt near Dusty's feet. "El Guapo only kills men, he does not kill crying women," he told them scornfully. "So go, you big movie stars. . . ." He gave the last words a vicious twist as he pointed to the horizon.

Lucky, Dusty, and Ned did not have to be told twice. They backed away humbly from his presence, bowing from the waist again and again until they reached their horses. Then, leaping into their saddles, they swiftly rode away, heading for the edge of town. As they passed the people of Santo Poco, the outraged villagers turned their faces away.

But The Three Amigos were riding too fast to see the tears in Carmen's eyes, the disappointment on Rodrigo's young face, or the deep sorrow that cut lines in Papa Sanchez's cheeks and brow.

El Guapo threw back his head and laughed victoriously, like a coyote howling over a piece of dead meat. "Faster!" he shouted, drawing his pistols and firing them into the air. "Faster!"

Spurring their horses hard, The Three Amigos took off faster than three rabbits chased by a fox. Behind them, they could hear the vicious laughter of the gleeful *ban-*

didos, but at this moment Lucky, Dusty, and Ned were beyond shame, beyond humiliation. They were glad to be alive, and they wanted to keep it that way.

But now the fun part was over.

El Guapo had ceased to be amused, and his ugly laughter died away, replaced by a ferocious scowl. "People of Santo Poco," he shouted. "You were very foolish to bring these men to try to stop El Guapo. You have hurt me." His eye fell on the lovely Carmen Sanchez, who was weeping brokenheartedly on her father's shoulder, and he leered.

"Shall we kill everyone?" asked the ferret-faced Jefe eagerly, his hand already on his pistol butt.

The bandit leader shook his head. "No, Jefe, we do not kill the hens before they lay the eggs," he grinned. "You see, Jefe, the harvest is not yet in. If we kill everyone, we will have to gather the crops ourselves."

This made sense, even to the trigger-happy Jefe.

Now El Guapo's icy gaze swept the villagers, and they shuddered in fear. They knew that they had made a boo-boo of monumental proportions, and that El Guapo would make them pay for it, triple damages. It would not go easy on the people of Santo Poco. Those *bandidos* would teach them a lesson that every farming village in this part of Mexico would learn from.

El Guapo could not keep his eyes off Carmen Sanchez. He liked his women beautiful and terrorized; female weeping turned him on. This little filly appealed to him more and more as he gazed upon her tear-stained loveliness. "*Buenas dias, señorita,*" he cooed at her, taking off his hat with a flourish.

Carmen averted her face; she could not bear the look of malevolent triumph in his eyes. Guilt and sorrow racked her; all of this was her fault. She alone was to blame. If only she had not gone into that church in Diablo! Yet even now, even when The Three Amigos had fled like the chickenhearts they were, she couldn't help remembering Lucky Day as she had first seen him on that makeshift movie screen — so dashing, so brave, so handsome! It was a double and triple burden of grief-stricken regret that Carmen had to bear.

"You see, Jefe, a rose *can* bloom in the desert," laughed El Guapo. And before her father could raise a horrified hand to stop him, the bandit had swooped down like a falcon and seized the girl, lifting her onto his saddle and pinning her there with one strong arm.

Carmen kicked and struggled to escape, but her screams fell on deaf ears and the girl's attempts at resistance only made El Guapo more delighted with his stolen prize. Boy, was he a mean mother!

Holding Carmen tight with one hand, he drew a bound bundle of dynamite sticks from his saddlebag with the other and lit the fuse at the glowing tip of his cigarillo. When the fuse was burning well, he threw the bundle to his second in command.

"The town is yours, *muchachos*," he cried. "Jefe! Santo Poco is no longer under my protection!"

Jefe uttered a wild whoop of delight and, waving the bundle of dynamite like a banner over his head, he rode straight for the church.

The church! The villagers shrieked in dismay. Who in his right mind blows up a church? *No es posible*. Nevertheless, there it went. Holy smithereens exploded everywhere as the church was reduced to a pile of sanctified rubble in the flicker of an eye.

For the *bandidos*, the destruction of the church was their signal. Like the barbarians at the sack of Rome, they rode through the town in all directions, putting buildings to the torch, firing their pistols at innocent chickens, running down livestock and villagers alike with the pounding hooves of their frenzied horses. Take my word for it; it was a bad scene.

In fifteen bloodcurdling minutes it was all over; Santo Poco had been pounded within an inch of its life. This would go down forever in the annals of Santo Poco history as Black Wednesday. Why, nobody would ever know, because today was Thursday. But let it pass. The good news is that El Guapo and his men, having their fun, rode out of the village, leaving the Santo Pocanos to pick up the pieces.

The bad news is that he took Carmen Sanchez with him as his prisoner.

The hoofbeats had died away at least ten minutes before The Three Amigos emerged from their hiding place. They had spent the destructive quarter of an hour crouching terrified behind their horses, out of sight under the ridge of a tufted dune. Now they crept out silently and brushed themselves off the best way they could. They didn't dare meet one another's eyes.

Slowly, cautiously, Lucky, Dusty, and Ned entered the village. Wreckage, devastation, and havoc was the scene everywhere. What a nightmare! Ground zero. Some of the houses were still burning, while others had already been reduced to rubble. Broken doors and smashed windows lay like charred corpses in the street. Hopelessly, some of the villagers were attempting to put out the fires, while others were collecting the remains of the animals, both dead and alive. What had once been the prosperous little farming village of Santo Poco was now a smoldering ruin.

The Three Amigos made their way slowly down the main street, smiling uncertainly and waving to whichever villager caught their eye. But the Santo Pocanos turned away from them in disgust, and mothers snatched up their children, lest the gaze of the three despicable cowards bring the *ninos* bad luck. Whatever popularity they might have enjoyed at last night's fiesta had totally vanished. But such is fame. One minute they're all over you; the next, you can't get anybody on the phone.

The Sanchez house was still standing, although it had taken a bad beating. Windows had been smashed out, and the flowering vines, ripped from their supporting trellis, lay in dying ruins upon the ground. Dismounting, The Three Amigos knocked at the door. That is, Lucky did the knocking, but it was really for all of them.

Papa Sanchez opened the door of his casa and scowled at them. Behind him, Mama Sanchez was weeping into her apron loud, choking sobs.

Dusty and Ned pushed Lucky forward as their spokesman.

"Is he gone?" Lucky asked in a half whisper.

"Yes, he is," wept *Mamacita*.

A sigh of relief escaped all three Amigos. "We'll just get our things and go," said Dusty.

"There is nothing of yours here," retorted Papa Sanchez coldly. "El Guapo has taken everything."

"Sorry," said little Ned sincerely.

"Yeah, me too," added Dusty Bottoms. "Say, did you happen to see a pair of cuff links? They were mother-of-pearl . . ."

"Dusty!" Lucky held up one hand to cut him off. "Where's Carmen?" he asked the Sanchezes.

"El Guapo has taken her, too. By now they are well on their way to Mission Escorial. We may never see her again."

The door slammed shut in their faces. For a minute or two the three said nothing, for what was left to say? None of this was their fault; how could it be? They were entertainers, not heroes. The Three Amigos were a fiction created on celluloid, not men of flesh and blood. Underneath their costumes they were just three out-of-work actors who thought they'd had a good gig going. It was all a misunderstanding; they had never claimed to be heroes, never claimed to be anything but what they were. Just Lucky Day, Dusty Bottoms, and Ned Nederlander — lovers, not fighters. Song-and-dance men, not gunslingers.

And yet . . .

And yet . . . in other times, in other places, in other circumstances, what might they not have accomplished? No, it didn't bear thinking about. Put it out of your minds, Amigos, and get your asses out of there. Before it's too late.

There were no explanations to be made, no apologies. After all, none of this was their fault. Yet, when Dusty spotted little Umberto Rodriguez, six years old, standing forlornly near his burned-out *casa*, he felt he had to explain. Kneeling in the dust next to the child, he spoke softly.

"Umberto, many years from now, when you become a man, you'll realize that sometimes for a man to really be a man, he must act as if he were not a man. And because we are men, for us it took more courage to act unmanly than it would have taken other men less manly than we, men who might probably have acted more like real men. You do understand, don't you? When there's nothing we can do . . ." He broke off, just as confused by his own explanation as the child was. Somehow the thought had gotten away from him, and he was no longer positive that what he was saying was actually true. He stood up abruptly.

"Let's go," said Dusty quietly. He turned and headed for the horses.

"Yeah," agreed Lucky. "Let's go back to Hollywood. I think I can find our way back to the train station."

"The sooner the better," said Dusty.

"It's too hot down here," said Lucky.

"Bad on my hay fever," said Dusty.

"We don't belong down here," said Lucky.

Dusty's face softened, and his eyes took on a faraway expression. "Funny . . . they really seemed to like the first show. The second show didn't go so well . . ."

They had reached the horses. "Where's Ned?" asked Lucky, suddenly realizing that Ned Nederlander had taken no part in their conversation.

The two of them turned to see Ned several yards behind

them, his lips set tightly together, a look of determination making his small face grim. He was strapping on his gunbelt.

"What're you doing, Ned?" asked Lucky.

"What have we got to go back to?" Ned asked bitterly. He broke open the chambers and began to load his pistols with live ammunition dropped by the bandits. "We've got no jobs, no money, no place to live, no friends, no women, no self-respect. . . ."

"Whoa!" cried Lucky and Dusty. They could see the dangerous path down which Ned's words were leading him.

"We could get killed!" protested Dusty.

But Ned was beyond caring about that, beyond fear itself. The stubborn look on his face intensified.

"Back there The Three Amigos are already dead. Here we could be The Three Amigos for real," he declared. "I'm drawing a line." With the toe of his boot, Ned drew a line in the dust. "Men or mice, what'll it be?" he challenged quietly.

A long moment dragged by while Ned stared soberly at Dusty and Lucky from his side of the line. It was evident that he wasn't kidding around. This was serious, even deadly business.

Lucky Day drew a deep breath, jammed his sombrero on his head, twirled his pistols jauntily, and stuck them back in their holsters. Then he stepped over the line and joined Ned. Now they were two Amigos, but they were still waiting for one more in order to be The Three Amigos.

They didn't have to wait long. Dusty Bottoms cleared his throat. He looked up at the sky, over at Ned and Lucky, then once more at the sky while he thought of something dramatic to say to heighten this suspenseful moment of decision. Not coming up with a line, he twirled his revolvers as Lucky had done and came very close to shooting himself in the foot. Then he, too, took the decisive step over the line.

So. Here they were, The Three Amigos once more.

And what now? Could life imitate art? Could they become in truth the heroes that they were in fiction? Maybe yes, maybe no, but there was no going back now. Mice or men — Ned had offered them the choice, and they had opted for men. Nobody was more surprised about it than The Three Amigos themselves.

They had witnessed the cold cunning of El Guapo, seen what he was capable of doing to an innocent village, with its innocent people and innocent chickens. They had no illusions, no expectations that it would be easy. This wasn't cinema; there were no cameras here, no director and no comfy dressing rooms. Nobody would yell "Cut!" when the going got rough. There was no being picked up in the limo at the end of the working day. They would be staring death in the face, and a damn ugly face it was, too.

How ugly was it?

Why, man, it was so ugly that . . . Never mind. No more horsing around. This is heavy-duty business. We're talking life and death here. Somewhere across that desert was the stronghold of El Guapo the vicious, ruled by a cold-blooded murderer and manned by an army of cut-throats and villains. There were only three of them against overwhelming odds, but they were not afraid.

Well . . . maybe just a little afraid. But they sucked in their guts, straightened their shoulders, stood as tall as they knew how, and gave the world the famous Three Amigos salute — one, two: hands crossed on chest; three: hands on hips. And that made them feel a whole lot better.

Side by side, they rode out together to do battle against evil, to right the wrong done to the people of Santo Poco. Like Ned Nederlander always said, "Wherever there is injustice you will find us; wherever there is suffering we'll be there."

Side by side they rode away.

And side by side they rode back again five minutes

later — to get directions. They had no idea where the hell they were supposed to be going.

Hours afterward, exhausted and hungry, The Three Amigos made camp. Night had stolen over the desert, and the air was cold. A high, pale moon lent illumination to the darkness and, somewhere not very far away, a pair of lonesome coyotes sang a mournful song to it. Somehow Lucky and Dusty had managed to get a small campfire going, feeding it with dried sticks and bits of desert tumbleweed. Ned, the marksman, had gone off to shoot some dinner and had returned successful, his pockets bulging.

The Three Amigos sat shivering as close to the fire as they dared, roasting their food on small spits made of green twigs broken off a Joshua tree. As dinner was cooking, Dusty strummed a few chords on his guitar. Even flat and off-key, the music made the night somehow more gentle, more hospitable.

"Great job catching the food, Ned."

"Thanks, Lucky." Ned blushed at the praise. "How do you like your bat, Dusty?"

"Medium rare, thanks."

Ned reached over the fire carefully and removed one of the roasting bats from its improvised spit. He handed it over to Dusty, who began munching on a leathery wing.

"I'll tell you something," said Lucky quietly as he laid down his dinner, "I think this is the best decision we ever made. This is the challenge of our lives."

"I'm going to have to give the performance of my career," declared Ned with something very like enthusiasm.

"Dusty, you're going to be doing your stunts for real."

"No problem," answered Dusty lightly. "Lucky, do you want your wings?"

"No, I've had enough, thanks. Here. You know, Amigos, we may have to kill some people," Lucky said.

"Huh?" Ned reacted.

"You mean shoot at *people*?" Dusty's voice cracked in alarm.

"Sure," replied Lucky. "It's killed or be killed. You've killed people before, haven't you, Dusty?"

"Me? Yeah, sure . . . sure I have. Not many."

"So have all of us," said Lucky. "I've killed a few. You, too, eh, Ned?"

Ned hesitated. "Oh . . . yeah . . . well, I've killed a few. Wounded mainly. But sure, yeah."

There was a long silence as each of them stared into the firelight, each of them reflecting that all of them were liars. Killing people; that was heavy. Killing was like *permanent*. Would The Three Amigos be up to it? *Quién sabe?* Only tomorrow would tell.

"Well," said Lucky at last, sighing deeply, "we've got a busy day ahead of us tomorrow. We'd better turn in." He glanced across at Ned Nederlander, whose eyes were already closed. "Look at the little fella. Tuckered out already."

Somewhere nearby a coyote howled. Ned's eyes snapped open. "What was that?" he quavered.

"Just a coyote. Take it easy, Ned."

"Well, I've never slept outside before."

"Sing him a song, Dusty."

Dusty Bottoms picked up his guitar and ran his fingers lightly across the strings. In a soft voice, he sang young Ned a western lullaby. Little Ned relaxed slowly and let his eyelids drift shut. The man in the moon looked down in surprise at this unlikely trio of heroes, and the desert winds died down to let them sleep warm.

"Good night, Lucky."

"Good night, Dusty."

"Good night, Ned."

The Three Amigos are sleeping soundly in the moonlight while tall cactuses guard them and the desert floor offers a sandy pillow for their tired heads. And not a single one of them is dreaming that death awaits them, death beckons to them tomorrow.

Chapter Ten

Mission Escorial was getting ready for fiesta.

"Fiesta" is the Mexican peasant's middle name. *Mexicanos* are party animals. If it's a saint's day, they hold a fiesta. If the cat has kittens, they hold a fiesta. If they should actually happen to know who the kittens' father was, there is yet another fiesta. Well, why not? They are an honest, hardworking people, so why shouldn't they let off a little steam now and then with some music and some dancing and a lot of wine and tequila?

But this fiesta was different. On the surface, it was the customary annual celebration of the natal day of the great hero of the Mexican people, El Guapo the *bandido*. His birthday was always the occasion for flowing booze and accommodating women. All day long, the piñatas had been pouring in to Mission Escorial. Villagers had carried them in on burros and even on their backs. And still they were coming, to be piled up in a shed under the watchful eye of Jefe.

Every year the peasants under El Guapo's reign of terror sent him gifts. Or, rather, gifts were extorted from them under threats of maiming or death. So every village in the locality chipped in and got him birthday presents.

Mexican gift wrapping is really quite sensational. Each present is wrapped in many layers of colorful tissue paper, then a group of gifts is assembled and all of them are enclosed in a brightly painted papier-mâché covering called a piñata. Piñatas can be any shape or size; some are in the form of animals, such as a purple cow or a red burro or a bright green chicken, while others are less ambitious but no less attractive — round, square, rhomboidal, heptagonal, hemi-elliptical, and so forth.

The idea is to string these piñatas up high, just out of reach. They are fastened with strong, heavy ropes attached to a wall, and they dangle overhead about seven or eight feet from the ground. Then the birthday boy is blindfolded and whirled round and round until he is almost dizzy. A stick is placed in his hands and he must lumber around blindly, trying to break the piñatas with his stick, so that the many little presents tumble down and hit him on the head.

Once in a while a peasant braver than most would pack a giant rock in his piñata, hoping that it would crack open El Guapo's skull when it fell. He could have saved himself the trouble, because El Guapo never allowed himself to be blindfolded. His eyes were always open and always on his men, for he didn't trust a single one of them, and with good reason. He played the piñata game his own way; he just had others doing the blindfold act with a stick, and he collected the presents. If anybody was hit on the head, it wasn't El Guapo.

Preparations for the party were in full swing. Colorful lanterns made of oiled paper were being strung across the courtyard, to be lit this evening for the dancing after the sun went down. The cooks had risen very early, to turn out birthday tortillas and enchiladas for two hundred guests. An ox was already roasting on a giant spit near the smokehouse. It was expected to be some shindig.

To all appearances the occasion for this fiesta was to celebrate El Guapo's birthday. But there was another, darker purpose, something El Guapo had been keeping to himself. Even Jefe didn't have an inkling of what had been going on.

El Guapo was restless. For years he had been terrorizing the countryside, and in the end what had it brought him? True, he lived like a king in a castle, with everything a villain could want. But outside of this tiny corner of Mexico, who had ever heard of El Guapo? Even the *federales* were half-hearted in their pursuit; catching El Guapo would hardly make them national heroes. Not like Pancho Villa.

Pancho Villa! Now *there* was a bandit! Half the police force in Mexico was on his trail; even the *americanos* kept sending soldiers after him, because he was always raiding north of the border, too. What was the name of El Guapo compared with that of Pancho Villa? *Nada*. Zero. Señor Anonymity.

But El Guapo had plans, secret plans. He was getting ready to expand his operation and to make his appearance on the national scene. Soon the name of El Guapo would make the entire country sit up and take notice. He had formed a secret alliance with an evil German, who had promised him the most advanced and deadly weapons in exchange for half of Mexico. Soon his men would throw away their ancient Enfields, Springfields, and Brownings. They would have the most up-to-date rifles and automatic pistols. They would enjoy machine guns that could spit out a hundred bullets a second. They would even have aeroplanes. The German had promised him aeroplanes to deal death from the skies. El Guapo could hardly wait to get his hands on those.

Today the German would attend the fiesta, and see for himself El Guapo's importance and power. The agreement would be sealed, and El Guapo would make the announcement to his bandits. Then recruitment would begin. With powerful new weapons, El Guapo would raise a bandit army the likes of which Mexico had never experienced. He would write a new chapter in the history of wickedness.

Then El Guapo would be undefeatable. He would no longer have to depend on the local peasantry for food, and he would smash them all. Beginning with and especially Santo Poco, which had dared to bring in three gringo monkeys, three stupid clowns to stand up to him. In the old days such an act of defiance would have called down total destruction. Their mangy village would have been burned to the ground and all its people killed. They must now be thinking that El Guapo was getting soft. Soft, eh? He would show them soft!

Yes, today would be a very special birthday. With much tequila, many women, and many piñatas filled with gifts. But one special gift he had reserved for tonight. Yes, tonight he would "unwrap" that pretty package from Santo Poco, Carmen Sanchez. He chuckled evilly at the thought, and his cigarillo stood straight up in the air. He could hardly wait for the festivities to begin.

In a locked bedroom deep in the heart of the mission, Carmen Sanchez slept the fitful sleep of total exhaustion. When she had been brought to this room the day before, a smelly and unshaven bandit had dumped her unceremoniously onto the wide bed and left her to yell her head off is she chose. So she did. She screamed for help until her throat was raw, and pounded on the heavy iron-studded oaken door until her small fists were bleeding, but nobody came.

At last, worn out and terrified, she looked around at her surroundings and her brows lifted in surprise. This place was more like a church than a bedroom. Religious pictures hung everywhere on huge bronze hooks, and statues of saints stood in niches carved into the stucco walls. Against the far wall stood a little shrine to the Holy Virgin, and Carmen threw herself on her knees before it, imploring the Mother to free her from this terrible imprisonment. She remained there for what seemed to her like hours, praying with her arms around the base of the statue and her head resting on the Virgin Mary's feet.

But her prayers went unanswered, and nobody came to unlock the door and set her free. Her head ached with weeping, and she longed for rest. But the sight of the huge carved bed made Carmen shudder. She didn't dare to think of what fate might be awaiting her at the hands of the hideous El Guapo.

A long table stood in the middle of the large room; on it was a jug of crude wine and half a loaf of bread. Carmen rose from the shrine with shaky knees and went to the table. She took a few sips of the wine and ate a little of the bread. Then weariness overcame her at last and, worn out by the events and emotions of the day, she sank into restless sleep. She was still sitting in the chair, her head pillowed on her outstretched arm, which rested on the table, the following morning.

That was the way Maria Elena found her when she unlocked the door and came in with Carmen's breakfast.

Maria Elena put down the tray of food and glanced sharply at the girl. Even with swollen eyes and tear-stained cheeks, even with her hair straggling from the confines of the modest knot she always wore, Carmen Sanchez was very beautiful.

"Today is El Guapo's birthday, and tonight you are to be El Guapo's woman," said Maria Elena, not unkindly.

The girl's face paled, but her eyes flashed defiance. "I would rather die!"

Where have I heard that before? thought Maria Elena with a tinge of bitterness, remembering that time long ago when she herself had been just as young and just as beautiful, and that she herself had been kidnapped from her village and brought here. "Let me prepare you for the way El Guapo makes love. Carmen, do you know what foreplay is?"

Carmen's eyes widened in fear. "N . . . no," she quavered.

"Good. Neither does El Guapo."

The Three Amigos had been riding for hours. They had no idea a desert could be this big or this empty. Or this dangerous. Rattlesnakes lay coiled beneath every rock; sandstorms lurked around every corner (if a desert may be said to have corners). They were hungry, they were thirsty, but they didn't dare to dismount. Who knew what perils awaited them if they tried to make camp? There wasn't a drop of water anywhere in sight.

Ned Nederlander remembered from his Boy Scout Handbook that every cactus holds within its pulpy flesh a veritable fountain of cool, sweet water. But after two attempts to get at it, resulting in thousands of painful little prickles in all of his fingers and the palms of his hands, Ned said the hell with it, which was very strong language indeed for little Ned.

Now, after many miles of arid desert, the terrain was at last beginning to change. The sand and shale and dried-up beds of abandoned arroyos, the endless procession of cactus trees like prickly sentinels, were giving way to rock and scrub pine. No more desert dwellers, no more lizards, scorpions, or treacherous sidewinders; now they saw foxes and trundling badgers and, once, a lion club. They were climbing, the rocks becoming foothills, the foothills giving promise of mountains barely glimpsed now over the horizon. Even the air was different. It was thinner and much cooler, no longer the stifling, stagnant breath of desert heat.

According to the directions, Mission Escorial must not be much farther off. They were getting close. Soon they would actually be there — and then what?

For hours Lucky, Dusty, and Ned had journeyed without speaking, each of them silently wrapped in his own thoughts. What lay ahead of them was too momentous a task for words. When the time came, they would have to be ready. That's all there was to it. Until then, The Three Amigos merely took comfort from the quiet presence of one another.

The noise of an engine directly overhead cut through the air. What the hay?

"It's the Tubbman 601 we saw in Diablo," said Ned, pointing up at the German's biplane, which was just now passing above them, flying low enough so that the three could read the registration numbers on the side. Now its nose dropped, and it began a landing approach, circling slowly in a descending arc.

"He must be going to El Guapo's," said Lucky thoughtfully. "Huh."

What was the aeroplane doing here? Who was flying it? Was this airship something The Three Amigos should know about? Was it some missing piece of the perilous puzzle which they'd have to deal with at the mission?

One good thing, though. If this plane *was* landing at El Guapo's hideout — and where else would it be landing? — it meant that The Three Amigos were on the right track and the bandit stronghold was exactly where they thought it would be. They followed the arc of the plane, watching to see where it landed, and turned their horses in that precise direction.

Jefe sat mounted on his horse, a clipboard and yellow lead pencil in his hands, supervising the delivery of the piñatas. When El Guapo had seized the Jesuit mission for his own, he'd had huge walls built all the way around it, securing it from outside approach. Made of stone, the walls soared high above the mission itself. The only entrance was through a pair of massive iron gates set into the wall, and they were always locked and barred.

Only today, the day of the birthday, were the gates allowed to open frequently and freely to admit the farmers inside with their gifts. Nevertheless, armed men stood on guard everywhere; El Guapo never took chances.

Another piñata, a large, round yellow one like the sun arrived, only this sun was painted with pink and purple polka dots. Truly a thing of beauty! Carrying it slung between them, a pair of sweating peasants staggered through the gates.

"This piñata is a gift from the people of Puerta Rosa."

"What a beautiful piñata," approved Jefe. "El Guapo will be pleased. Take it into the storeroom and put it with the others."

A flurry of hoofbeats made the bandit turn around. El Guapo the birthday boy was riding up, dressed in a brand-new suit but the same old sombrero.

"Jefe!" he called. "Has the German arrived yet?"

"Not yet, El Guapo," saluted Jefe. "But many presents have been coming for your birthday."

The bandit leader gave a disdainful shrug and a dismissive wave of the hand. The piñatas interested him not at all; he knew what they would contain. More *huraches*, more handwoven serapes, little straw souvenir donkeys, and hand-painted clay figurines of saints. Bah, tourist trash! "The German has the only presents I want. Guns. Guns so that the name of El Guapo will be hanging on everyone's lips!"

"He will be here, El Guapo," Jefe reassured his boss. "But I think you will like your other presents, too. I have put many beautiful piñatas in the storeroom. Each of them is filled with little surprises."

A malicious gleam appeared in the bandit chieftain's eye. "Many piñatas?" he asked Jefe coyly.

Jefe should have recognized the tone and suspected the trap, but that boy never learned. He was always a sucker for El Guapo's nasty little jokes and games. That's no doubt why he managed to hold on to his job as second in command despite his monumental incompetence.

"Oh, yes, many," he answered happily.

"Would you say," continued El Guapo slyly, "that I have a plethora of piñatas?"

"A what?" Nobody home.

"A plethora."

Mulling it over, Jefe realized that he was lost and that faking it was probably the best if not the only solution. "Oh, yes, you have a plethora," he nodded, suspecting nothing.

El Guapo sprung the trap. "Jefe, what is a plethora?"

Jefe closed his eyes and swallowed hard. He'd been suckered and now his ass was going to be hung out to dry. "Why, El Guapo?" he croaked feebly.

"Well, you told me I had a plethora," said El Guapo with a darkening brow, as he rose in his saddle the better to shout at this idiot, "and I would just like to know what a plethora *is*. I would not like to think that a person would tell someone he has a plethora and find out that that person had no idea what it means to have a plethora!" By the time he was finished, the veins were pulsing in El Guapo's forehead.

Jefe took a wild guess; what did he have to lose anyway? "Does it mean 'many'?"

The boss bandit's brows shot up in surprise. "Why, yes. Tell me, Jefe, how did you know?"

"Just lucky, I guess. Forgive me, El Guapo. I know I do not have your superior intellect and education, but it could be that once again you are angry at something else and are looking to take it out on me?"

Bull's-eye. El Guapo scowled and said nothing, but his silence was eloquent admission.

"Could it be because you are turning forty today?"

A low growl escaped the leader's throat, and Jefe wisely decided to stay off that subject. "Could it be because Carmen chooses to sleep in the cell instead of with you?"

El Guapo shrugged and muttered something under his breath, and Jefe took that to be a signal of agreement.

"Then why do you not just take her? When you want cattle, you take the cattle. When you want food, you take the food. When you want a woman, you just take the woman. Why do you not just take her?"

El Guapo smiled expansively. "You do not understand women," he purred, a man of the world. "You cannot force open the petals of a flower. When the flower is ready, it opens itself up to you."

Jefe grinned a knowing grin. "And when do you think Carmen will open up her flower to you?"

"Tonight . . . or I will kill her!"

El Guapo's romantic mood was interrupted by the sound of an aeroplane engine. Looking up, he saw the Tubbman 601 circling in low for a landing. "There is the German now. Right on time. We must make him welcome." He turned his horse's head and rode away, his mind fixed on the serious and deadly business ahead. His thoughts now were all of guns, beautiful guns. The girl could wait.

"This ought to do it. Let's stop here."

Dusty Bottoms, Lucky Day, and Ned Nederlander got down from their horses, their tushies aching to the bone. What a trip! The Three Amigos stretched for a minute, trying to get all the kinks out; they'd been riding for so long they'd forgotten what earth felt like underfoot. It felt rocky, but welcome all the same.

Looping the horses' reins over the branch of a tree, Lucky looked around, spying the nearby edge of a ridge.

"This way, boys."

The Three Amigos approached the rim of the ridge with the utmost caution. If their calculations were correct, they ought to be directly above El Guapo's mountain fortress, and they didn't want to take any chances of being spotted and shot on sight.

Dropping to their knees, The Three Amigos peeked over the top of the ridge and took their first look at Mission Escorial.

"My God!" whispered Dusty, appalled.

El Guapo's mountain stronghold was like nothing they had imagined. It wasn't a hideout, it was a fully armed encampment, and it housed literally hundreds of badmen. On the long ride from Santo Poco all they could think about was redeeming their honor, rescuing Carmen Sanchez, and spitting in El Guapo's eye. They'd never discussed exactly *how* they intended to do any of this, and they'd *certainly* never discussed what to do if faced with a fort and an army. Perhaps they should have, but you can't always think of *everything*.

"We've got to figure out a way to get inside," mused Lucky. His brow furrowed in thought.

"It looks impossible," answered Ned.

"Lucky, those walls are twenty-five feet high," Dusty pointed out. "There are guards at every post. There's no way we'll ever get in there."

"I think Dusty's right," Ned agreed reluctantly. It did seem hopeless.

"We're going to have to use our brains," Lucky declared.

Ned and Dusty exchanged horrified glances and moaned, aghast. Surely there must be some other way! Surely they could do better than that!

"All right," said Lucky, lowering his voice to a confidential whisper. "Here's my plan. . . ."

They bent their heads to listen, and a buzzard, high on the rocks overhead, saw them, and from past experience, began to lick its chops. Dinner was almost ready, and it looked delicious.

Chapter Eleven

Naturally, the most crucial part of the plan was for The Three Amigos to stick together and not allow themselves to become separated. Together they'd have one another to depend on; they'd be able to wield a shared strength. As three separate individuals, they could only be weak, helpless, and doomed.

So of course the very first thing that happened was that they got separated.

But let's not get ahead of our story.

A jubilant El Guapo had sent Jefe with the buckboard and a pair of hitched mules out to the aeroplane, to bring back the German and the guns. The bandit leader could hardly contain his excitement while he waited; his eyes glittered with malevolent glee, and his breath came rasping from his chest. His smile was not lovely to behold. When he was most happy, that's when El Guapo was at his ugliest. Boy, was he ugly!

How ugly was he?

Oh, all right. Why, man, he was so ugly that when he looked into the bathroom mirror, the mirror in the *bedroom* broke, too.

At last he could hear the creaking of the buckboard wheels outside the walls, and the signal was given. Two badmen opened the iron gates, and in drove Jefe. El Guapo saw with elation that the buckboard was piled high with wooden crates and that the German was sitting next to the bandit on the buggy seat. Two strangers in well-cut suits sat on the packing cases.

"Zese men are my compatriots," explained the German, climbing down. "Ve do business together."

The two men clicked their heels and bowed sharply from the waist in Teutonic greeting. El Guapo narrowed his eyes; he trusted nobody, and least of all men he'd never seen before. Germans were not his top priority. Weapons were.

"Jefe!" he called.

Jumping down from the buckboard, Jefe picked up a crowbar and attacked the topmost crate. "Here come the guns, El Guapo," he chortled.

"Let me see." The *bandido* boss crowded forward, peering into the case. Then he threw his head back and uttered a long, terrible-sounding laugh of triumph. A dozen brand-new rifles with long, menacing barrels were lying in a bed of straw, packed in oil, like death-dealing Portuguese sardines.

"Show me," he commanded. The German reached in and pulled out one of the new Garands, dirtying his hands with machine oil, which he impatiently wiped off with a rag. He cleaned the rifle down until the black barrel gleamed, then opened it and loaded it with long cartridges. The bolt clicked sharply in the crisp mountain air. The German sighted down the barrel.

"Give me that," cried El Guapo eagerly, taking the gun into his own hands. "Let me see how it works." He was like a child with a new toy.

Whirling around, El Guapo looked for a target. He

spotted one of the guards in the watchtower on top of the wall. "What's his name?" he asked Jefe.

"Paco."

"Paco," yelled the bandit leader, "hold out your hat!"

The badman grinned okay and took off his sombrero, holding it out for El Guapo to shoot at. El Guapo squinted down along the barrel, aimed carefully, then fired.

Paco clutched his chest and pitched forward off the wall, quite dead.

"Hmmmm," muttered El Guapo. "Here," and he handed the rifle to Jefe. "Get this sight fixed." To the German he said, "You have lived up to your promise, *hombre*. You and your two friends here will be my guests at the celebration today. A little party my men are throwing for me," he added complacently.

Meanwhile, Lucky, Dusty, and Ned had embarked on the greatest adventure of their lives, their first live appearance as The Three Amigos in action. And without a rehearsal.

In order to get inside the mission, they had to climb over the surrounding high stone wall, at a point where there was no guard tower or sentry to stop them. This in itself would take some doing. The only place where the wall was unguarded was of course at the point at which it was almost impossible to scale.

The three of them sneaked along the base of the wall, looking for a likely spot to begin climbing. At last they reached a place where a rushing stream, running parallel to the mission, had piled up debris of boulders and rough stones at the base of the wall, giving them a leg up. They began to scramble up the rocks, getting in one another's way. Dusty, never the most agile of men, tripped over a stone and landed in the water up to his knees, and Ned kept barking his shins on the sharp edges of the rocks. But at last they reached the top. Now for the wall itself.

The wall had a crack in it, thanks to erosion by the

stream, and the crack afforded a couple of toeholds. First Lucky and Dusty tried to boost Ned up, but Ned's little hands kept slipping, so Lucky decided to go it alone. He got about halfway up the face of the wall and stopped. There was nowhere else he could go. Above him and around him the rock had turned smooth; Lucky discovered that he couldn't move in any direction except down. He was hanging spread-eagled against the rock face by the tips of his fingers.

"Hang in there, Lucky," called Dusty and Ned. "Don't let go."

"'Don't let go'? Oh, that's beautiful! That's just terrific! What the hell kind of advice is 'don't let go'? Just get me out of this!" Lucky shrieked.

"Coming!" promised Dusty. "I'm coming just as soon as I can figure out how. Just be quiet or they'll hear us."

Squatting down on the wall, Dusty thought long and hard. Over to his right, not far from Lucky, small branches were growing out between the stones of the wall. Some young saplings had taken root and were making an effort to survive. If the roots went deep enough, and if they would bear the weight of a small man, Ned could hand-over-hand up to the top of the wall by the branches, shin over to where Lucky was hanging, and pull him up to safety.

"I can't haul Lucky," protested Ned. "I'm too small. He weighs thirty pounds more than I do. *You* try it."

Dusty grimaced nervously. "I'm not sure those branches will hold me. But I'll give it the old college try."

"And hurry it up, if you don't mind," yelled Lucky anxiously. "I'm not getting any younger, and it's not as easy as it looks, hanging on here like a side of beef in a butcher-shop window."

With sweat dripping into his eyes from under his sombrero, Dusty inched slowly up the side of the wall, clinging to the jutting branches. Once or twice his hands slipped, and he almost fell, but still he managed to hang on. In less than three minutes, he was on top of the wall.

"Well, I'll be a monkey's uncle!" he grinned. "It worked! It actually worked!" Crouching down, he ran across the top of the wall to where Lucky was dangling about four feet from the summit.

"Hurry up!" Lucky cried urgently. "I can't hold on here much longer! My fingers have lost all feeling!"

Dusty lay down on his belly and reached over. "Okay, now start to let go. Gimme your right hand."

"Are you completely insane? If I let go, I'll fall on those rocks and smash into a million pieces!"

"Lucky, if you can show me how to get you up here without letting go, I'll take a stab at it. Until then, damn it, gimme your hand!"

Lucky squeezed his eyes shut so he wouldn't have to look and reached one hand up. He felt Dusty's strong hand clasping one, and then the other hand. Then there was a strong pull, and he was up on the wall beside Dusty Bottoms.

That made two out of three. But what about Ned?

"I'll be right with you," Ned called up in a loud whisper. He backed off about ten yards, took a long running start, and ran up the wall as nimbly as a mouse!

"When did you learn to do that?" gasped the other two Amigos, dumbfounded.

"That's a trick I did in *Little Neddy's Secret Adventure.* Well, we're all here. Now what?"

Good question. Crouching down as low as possible, The Three Amigos took a good look down at the courtyard. Below them, badmen were scurrying to and fro, setting up tables and stringing paper lanterns for what seemed to be a party. Musicians in broad sombreros and black velvet boleros were tuning up their instruments. Pretty women wearing off-the-shoulder blouses and ruffled skirts were carrying out huge platters of meat and bowls of black beans and yellow rice. Carmen Sanchez was nowhere to be seen.

Just beneath their feet, on the other side of the wall, were the ropes for the piñatas. Anchored firmly to large hooks embedded in the wall, the ropes dangled down. Some of the piñatas had already been fastened to rope ends and had been hauled up so that they dangled gaily over the courtyard like plump and painted kites. But other ropes had not yet been put to use. Three of them were free, the magic number.

The Three Amigos exchanged glances. Ropes — exactly what they needed. In every movie they'd made (with the sole exception of *Those Darn Amigos*) they had swung across some chasm or canyon or courtyard on ropes. Here indeed was life about to imitate the movies.

Without a word, each of them stooped down and gathered up a rope. With his left hand on the rope, each of them clenched his right fist upon his chest, over the heart, in a silent salute. Then they swung out into empty air.

The purpose of the operation was simple — the ropes were supposed to carry them across the courtyard, over the heads of the unsuspecting bandits, and land them lightly on the roof of the large building opposite. From there they could proceed with their plan of finding Carmen. She had to be locked up somewhere inside the mission itself. If nothing went wrong, it shouldn't be too hard to do.

But *only* if nothing went wrong.

The first thing that went wrong was that Lucky's rope was too long — way too long. Instead of flying through the air, he plunged straight downward and found himself being dragged across the courtyard, the toes of his boots making long, thin gouges in the dirt.

Ned's rope, on the other hand, was too short. He swung

hard, but nevertheless he didn't make it all the way across, so he had to swing back. But on the backswing his spurs got caught in one of the piñatas, and Ned Nederlander found himself hanging stretched across space, still clinging to the rope, with the courtyard a good ten feet below him.

Dusty's rope was just right. It propelled him all the way across the courtyard, in through a conveniently open window on the third floor of the mission, across a large bedroom, and smack between the open doors of a tall wardrobe, which closed with a bang, imprisoning him. He was still holding on to the rope. So much for landing on the roof.

But what Dusty didn't know was that this was the very room where Carmen Sanchez was being held prisoner. In fact, Carmen was still sleeping exhaustedly, her head pillowed on the wooden table. She didn't even hear the wardrobe doors slam shut.

However, the guard outside her room did. He came rushing in, his pistol drawn.

"What was that noise?" he demanded, waking up the girl.

Carmen raised her head groggily. "I do not know."

Luckily for Dusty, the guard didn't notice the end of the rope sticking out of the wardrobe. He merely gave a perfunctory look around and, grunting, went back to his post.

So The Three Amigos, who had vowed to stay together no matter what, were separated in the first minute of their first time out. Dusty locked in a closet, Ned doing a pretty fair impression of a piñata.

And Lucky?

Remember when you were a little kid and you played The Farmer in the Dell and somebody had to wind up as the Cheese Stands Alone in the center of the circle and nobody wanted to be the Cheese? Well, picture being the Cheese, only with a dozen hostile rifles loaded with live ammunition pointed directly at your head. That was Lucky Day, surrounded by El Guapo's men.

"So, we meet again, amigo," sneered the bandit chieftain.

Lucky raised his chin defiantly. "I have three demands," he stated. "One, that you stop harassing the people of Santo Poco. Two, that all the land of Mexico be redistributed equally among the peasants and that a system of proportional government be established, consisting of three separate but equal branches: a legislative, an executive, and a judicial. Three —"

Before Lucky could tell the bandits what his third demand was, El Guapo had grabbed him tightly by the throat and was squeezing hard enough to make Lucky's eyeballs bulge out parallel with his eyebrows.

"— Three," squeaked Lucky in a high, choked voice, "that the girl Carmen be returned to me unharmed."

El Guapo scowled heavily and pressed his ugly face so close to Lucky's that Lucky choked on the smoke from the bandit's cigarillo.

"Why did you come here?" demanded El Guapo. "You don't belong. Now we have to kill you. Take him away."

"Pardon me, did you say 'kill me'? Did El Guapo say 'kill me,' was that what he said?" Lucky's face turned ashen, and he whimpered a little as the bandits dragged him off. He didn't notice the German, who gave him a long, cold, speculative stare, as though trying to recall where he had seen this absurd American before.

Neither did he notice Ned Nederlander, who was still hanging over the courtyard, and whose arms were beginning to get a little tired. "So far, so good," muttered Ned to himself. *Even so, if only I had a plan! Any kind of plan would make me happier than this suspense. Suspense . . . suspense. . . . I'm up here suspended . . . get it? It's a joke.* But Ned didn't dare laugh, or he might let go and plunge to his death.

"Now you understand why I need your guns," El Guapo said to the German, shaking his head. "Jefe, the other two *yanquis* cannot be far away. They are annoying little flies. Swat them for me."

"*Sí*, El Guapo," giggled the delighted Jefe, who enjoyed nothing more than mayhem. "I'll swat them, with the greatest pleasure." Brandishing his sparkling new Garand rifle, he went off happily to try it out on real people. First he'd find them, then he'd shoot them.

The musicians finished tuning up and broke into a rollicking song. The party was about to begin.

"Come, German." El Guapo threw one arm around the scarred man's shoulders. "Now you and your friends here will enjoy the hospitality for which El Guapo is famous." The four strolled off to join the party.

Well, here's a fine mess The Three Amigos have gotten themselves into. Dusty Bottoms is locked in a goddamn closet. True, Ned is still hanging around, but soon, when it becomes time for the piñatas to be smashed to smithereens, one wouldn't want to be in Ned Nederlander's boots.

As for Lucky Day, he's just been dragged off, presumably to face a firing squad of brand-new rifles with sights that are just the teeniest bit off. Sounds like a slow and painful kind of death. Shooting like that will probably leave Lucky looking more like a spaghetti strainer than a movie star.

Is there a moral in any of this? Maybe it's "Don't crash parties. Wait until they send you an invite."

Chapter Twelve

Reluctantly, Carmen Sanchez dragged herself into wakefulness. Why even bother? Her situation was hopeless; she was still a prisoner in this locked room, still guarded by an armed desperado. Outside, she could hear the sounds of a party starting up. Music, laughter, dancing feet. Sounds that under other conditions would make the girl smile now caused her to shudder. She had no idea how many hours were left to her before El Guapo would enter this room and attempt to force his hideous self upon her, but she did know that time was slipping away from her quickly.

Was there nothing she could do to save herself from a fate worse than death? She looked around for a weapon to defend herself with, but there was nothing like that in the room. She considered breaking off a chair leg to use as a possible club, but the furniture was of solid oak, so heavy she couldn't even lift the chair, let alone break off one of its legs.

The thought of suicide actually crossed her mind, but she hastened to dismiss it. Carmen Sanchez was a religious girl, and suicide was a mortal sin; she would burn in hell forever. In her panic, she actually thought that perhaps she could hide so that El Guapo would never find her. But where? In this room there was nowhere to go ... unless ... that tall, heavy wooden wardrobe against the wall. ...

But what was that rope doing there? Carmen didn't remember seeing a rope leading into the closet before. Her heart in her mouth, she walked over to the wardrobe, threw the doors open, and gasped.

"Hi. Any mail for me?" asked Dusty Bottoms brightly.

"*Santa Maria!* Where did you come from? How on earth did you get in there?"

"It's a long story. No questions now; I'll tell you everything later. Right now we've got to get you out of here. First, you go get the horses and meet me out front."

"Good plan," approved Carmen. "But how? We can't even get out of this room. The door's locked, and there's an armed guard posted outside."

"Hmmmmmmmmm," said Dusty. "Let me think about it."

Oh, oh, sighed Carmen to herself. *If Dusty has to think, we're cooked.*

Lucky Day hadn't shut up yet. As the guards dragged him off to be locked up, to await the capture of the other Amigos for a triple execution, he was still babbling. "... See, under my system you would not be under the thumb of El Guapo," he told the guards, who continued to drag him across the courtyard. "You would be free to determine your own destiny.... You'd have the vote.... You'd even have a castle of your own...."

Ned's arms were getting real tired; how much longer he'd be able to hold on like this he had no idea. Below him, the party was heating up. There was music and laughter and feasting and dancing and much, much drinking. Each of the *bandidos* had been presented with a fresh bottle of tequila all to himself, and they were making good use of them. El Guapo was dancing with all the girls, one after the other. You know, that nasty *muchacho* wasn't such a bad dancer!

Any minute now they were going to remember the presents, and the birthday boy would be starting the piñata game. There's got to be a way out! Think, Ned, think!

"We Three Amigos have a plan," Dusty told Carmen.

"*Gracias a Dios.*" The girl smiled, relieved. "What is it?"

"First, we break into El Guapo's fortress."

"That you've done. Now what?"

Dusty's brows furrowed. "Well, we really didn't think the first part of the plan would work, so we have no further plan," he confessed. "Sometimes you can overplan these things. So, give me a second, I'll go talk to Lucky and get right back to you." He headed for the door.

"Wait! There's a guard outside the door, remember?"

"Oh, right." Dusty opened the door a crack and took a look. Carmen's guard was still sitting out there all right, but he had fallen asleep, his sombrero tilted over his face to keep out the light, his chair leaning backward against the wall. But even in his sleep, he held his rifle ready in his lap, with both hands wrapped protectively around the butt.

Dusty Bottoms drew his six-shooter and, followed by Carmen, he tiptoed out through the door and snuck up behind the guard's chair.

All Dusty had to do was hit him over the head hard enough to knock him out. Even so, he couldn't quite bring himself to do it; Dusty had never raised his hand against another human being in his entire life. Unless you counted a fight he had in third grade, a fight he'd lost by unanimous decision. He kept dancing around, making tentative passes with the butt of his pistol at the guard's sombrero. At last, he nerved himself to take a stab at it. He held the gun high and brought it down on the sleeping man's head, not hard enough to render the guard unconscious, merely enough to wake him up.

"What the —?" The guard began to get to his feet. The rifle barrel was pointing upward. His finger was tightening on the trigger. . . .

This was no time for squeamishness. Grabbing the six-shooter out of Dusty's hand, Carmen Sanchez slammed the butt down hard on the back of the guard's neck. With a low grunt, the bandit slumped to the floor, out like a light.

"Quick!" cried Carmen urgently. "You must dress in his clothing. Then you will be able to move freely in the courtyard."

"Good idea," said Dusty brightly. He took his gun back from the girl, gave it a showy twirl, and stuck it back into its holster. That hadn't gone so badly; Dusty Bottoms was feeling mighty pleased with himself.

Together they bent to take off the guard's serape. . . .

Two grinning *bandidos* escorted Lucky Day ungently to his cell. Not the best accommodations, in fact; actually more of a torture chamber than a prison.

In the days when the mission *was* a mission, the monks used to make and sell quite a palatable wine, which was stored in the cellar in huge barrels called hogsheads. They had devised a laborious but effective means of raising and moving these heavy hogsheads when they were filled. This involved a large winch and a pair of long weight-operated chains leading away from the winch, across the ceiling, and down through the opposite wall.

The winch had ratchets cut around its circumference, and the chains fitted into these ratchets. A pin in the winch regulated its movements and held the spring that controlled the counterweights so that the winch could revolve and the chains move either backward or forward, up or down, hoisting or lowering a barrel.

The device was designed to be operated manually by a lever from across the room, but pulling on the chains themselves would cause them to move along the ceiling, taking the hogshead with them. But why would anybody want to do it that way? It took enormous effort to pull on those chains without a lever, because of the heaviness of the counterweights. Only a very strong man would be able to do it at all.

Basically, it was your standard block-and-tackle pulley arrangement, with one or two refinements.

When El Guapo took over the mission, among the first items on his remodeling agenda was to adapt this fascinating block-and-tackle to the incarceration of poor, miserable prisoners. To the cell itself he added a barred door and a secure lock. He had wrist and ankle cuffs attached to the ends of the chains as shackles; once locked in them, the prisoner could be dragged backward and forward, up and down by the chains at the pleasure of his tormentor. It's surprising the amount of classified information a determined bandit leader was able to obtain quickly in this really rotten way.

With many a sniggering jest, the desperadoes attached the shackles to Lucky's ankles and wrists and gave the winch lever a quarter turn. The ancient machine creaked a bit rustily, but it still worked, and Lucky was dragged protesting across the cell's stone floor to the far wall. Another quarter turn of the lever and Lucky Day found himself hoisted a foot in the air and left hanging there, his arms and legs spread-eagled, pinned fast by the shackles.

Chuckling horribly, the *bandidos* dangled the keys to Lucky's chains, making them jingle. "Come and get them," laughed Juanito, the uglier of the two. He hung them on a hook right next to the winch lever. "Let us go, we

are missing the party. This one, he is not going anywhere
. . . *yet!*"

What a spot to be in, even more uncomfortable than
Duluth!

For a few minutes, Lucky Day just hung there, wondering what to do. Wondering, too, what had happened
to Dusty and Ned. He felt the sudden tug of anxiety
— would he ever see his best friends again? When he
closed his eyes, he could picture the impish grin that made
little Ned Nederlander so adorable and the puzzled look
that so often crept over Dusty Bottoms' face whenever
the conversation became hard to follow. He missed them,
dammit! Would The Three Amigos ever make another
motion picture?

It didn't seem likely, not with him dangling helplessly
from the ceiling and heaven only knew what was happening to the other two. And any minute those bandits
were no doubt going to come back and shoot him full
of holes. He was going to die! Suddenly Lucky Day's
customary confidence and cockiness evaporated like an
ice cube on a stove, and he just gave up, allowing the
anguish of black despair to rise up and engulf him. A
sob escaped and then another.

"How do I look?" asked Dusty, turning around so that
Carmen could get the whole effect.

"Fine! Let's go!"

"He wasn't really my size, and the pants are a little
short. But I think on the whole it's not too shabby. I
think the serape and sombrero will do the trick, don't
you?"

"Yes, yes!" the girl cried urgently. "But now we must
go! Somebody else may be coming along here at any
moment. Or the guard may wake up."

"Oh, right. Okay, you go for the horses. I'll take a
stroll and see what's happened to Lucky and Ned."

He ventured out cautiously, sidling down the corridor,

his eyes everywhere, his gun hand ready for anything. Except, perhaps, shooting.

In a few moments he had emerged from one of the floor-to-ceiling windows out onto a kind of gallery or balcony that ran around the outside of the building at second-floor level. From there he could get a good view of the courtyard below and the party in progress. This would be the perfect place to post a guard, he thought nervously.

But nobody barred Dusty's way; nobody came to challenge him. Just about every one of the *bandidos* was outside drinking and carousing at El Guapo's birthday party, which was now getting a little boisterous. Even the Germans were dancing with the women, and the level of liquid in the tequila bottles had dropped way, way down. Soon it would be time to sit down for the feasting and the toasting, after which the piñatas would be smashed and the presents opened, and one more El Guapo birthday celebration would be history.

Dusty made it safely down the stairs and out into the courtyard, disguising his face with the brim of his sombrero pulled as low as possible and the folds of his serape covering his chin. Nobody even noticed him; he was just another tall *bandido*. He wove quickly through the crowd of dancers and drinkers, his eyes peeled for Lucky or Ned.

If he'd only looked up above him for a second, he would have seen little Ned stretched across thin air, his face contorted with the effort of hanging on. Ned's legs were aching so badly from the strain that he didn't feel his spurs pulling a little loose from the piñata. He was *very* tired now, and his fingers were getting pretty numb. Soon there would be no feeling left in them, and then . . . watch out below!

After one or two minutes of wallowing in self-pity, Lucky stopped sniveling and began to pull himself together. It didn't take long for the old optimistic Lucky Day to snap back. The curtain wasn't down yet for the final bow, right? Where there was life, there was hope, right?

Across the room the keys to his liberty and continued existence were hanging tantalizingly on a hook, within plain sight. All he had to do was get to them, all he had to do was make the winch work without the lever.

He pulled hard on his chains, hoping to propel himself across the room. If he could balance the counterweights by his own weight and strength, Lucky might make the winch begin to turn all by itself. He might actually be able to hoist himself right over to those keys.

It was a long shot, it would be a bitch to do, but it was worth a try, because it was his only shot. He took a deep breath and strained again, and this time he was rewarded by the creaking noise the winch made as the ratchets began to slip. Again. Again. He moved half an inch . . . an inch . . . an inch and a half . . . Ah, good! His feet were touching the floor. Now for the really hard part.

"A toast to El Guapo!" cried Jefe, and the *bandidos* all cheered and waved their tequila bottles in the air. When Jefe stood up for the formal toast, the badmen came to attention, their eyes on their leader, who sat in the middle of the long table, the seat of honor, flanked by the Germans on both sides of him.

"*Salud!*" yelled the *bandidos*, "*Salud!* Good health to El Guapo!"

Pushing his way through the crowd of merrymakers, Dusty Bottoms was forced to stop where he was and raise a glass so he wouldn't stand out from the others. Unfortunately, when he stopped, Dusty was in the front rank of celebrants, almost opposite to El Guapo himself.

Who were those three strange-looking men sitting at the table with the bandit leader? One of them must be the pilot of that Tubbman aeroplane that The Three Amigos had followed, because he was costumed exactly like the fly-boy in every war movie Dusty had ever seen. Head to toe in leather, down to the leather helmet that hugged his ugly forehead. The flying goggles were pushed up on his brow, giving Dusty a look at that face. Brrrrrrr! Talk about mean! And that dueling scar didn't help make him any Mary Pickford, either. Three new players. What could that mean?

Jefe had prepared a little speech in honor of his boss. Raising his glass high, he began, "Today El Guapo is — "

A sharp glare from the bandit chief told him to cool it. El Guapo was not too thrilled about turning forty, and he might make somebody pay.

"— thirty-three years old. On behalf of myself and the rest of the boys, we chipped in and got you this gift."

Jefe nodded, and at his signal two badmen came running forward. Between them they were carrying a large gift-wrapped box tied with a red bow.

"No!" protested El Guapo, grinning in delight. "What did you *muchachos* go and do?!" He turned proudly to the Germans. "What can you say about such men?"

Eagerly grabbing the gift, he tore off the wrappings and opened the box. "Awwwwww. It's a sweater!"

"For when it gets a little cold at night," smiled Jefe.

El Guapo produced the present from its box for everybody to see and admire. It was a golfing sweater, a cardigan of many vivid colors with knitted-in wavy stripes and something vaguely resembling large polka dots or maybe soccer balls. Even judged by 1916 standards of knitwear, it was hideous.

"I love it!" The bandit leader threw his arms around Jefe and gave him a big hug. It was moments like these that bonded men together, moments like these that made El Guapo think twice about his *muchachos*. Maybe they *were* the best of the bunch after all.

"*Salud!*" cried the happy bandits. "*Viva El Guapo!*"

"*Viva,*" echoed Dusty Bottoms uncomfortably. He tried

to edge deeper into the crowd, but the enthusiastic partygoers kept jostling him farther forward. Now he was in the the very front row, practically under El Guapo's ugly nose. He hunkered down a little to look shorter; Dusty was at least five inches taller than your average *mexicano*. Even hunkered, though, he was beginning to feel mighty conspicuous.

The veins in Lucky's head and neck were standing out strongly and felt about ready to burst, but he continued to tug against his bonds. The ratchets had already slipped two or three notches, and the winch was beginning to turn, but every turn required a superhuman effort. Still, he was moving forward; only a tiny step at a time, but forward. At this rate he might reach those keys by sometime next Wednesday.

What it required was more strength, more concentration, bigger muscles. What it *really* required was two men and a lever. Lucky gritted his teeth and pulled even harder, although every muscle in his body was crying out for rest.

By now he had gained a few feet. Yes, he was definitely two or three feet closer to his goal. Lucky shook his head to clear the sweat from his eyes and took another painful step, followed by another.

SPROING!

The pulley device being more than two hundred years old, it was showing signs of wear. There was a nick in the next ratchet — not a large one, but large enough to resist the winch. A heartbeat of hesitation on the part of the pulley, and suddenly the spring controlling the weights moved the winch in the *counterdirection*.

With a surprised yelp, Lucky Day went flying backward through the air and ended up in his old position against the wall. Right back to square one.

Too bad, Lucky! But don't let it get you down. Nobody loves a quitter. When the going gets tough, the tough get going. If at first you don't succeed, try, try again.

Lucky, don't cry like that! Come on now, Lucky, get it together! Lucky? Lucky?

El Guapo was in an expansive mood, a marvelous mood, a mood compounded of birthday, tequila, and new rifles. Not to mention a pretty virgin locked in a room to be violated later, at his pleasure. Surrounded by his troops, his brand-new sweater draped fashionably around his shoulders, the sleeves dangling over his serape, El Guapo felt warm, loved, nostalgic. Also, he enjoyed making speeches.

"My men," he began, rising from his place at the table and going over to the rank and file who had been drinking to his health, "*mi compadres*, what we have done, we have done together." He walked down the line of *bandidos*, touching a shoulder here, bringing a gentle fist to a cheek there.

"I know each one of you like I know my own smell. Carlos" — El Guapo stopped to smile into the face of the man standing right next to Dusty Bottoms — "we fought together and rode together on many a raid. We fought priests, we fought farmers, we fought other *bandidos* who tried to muscle in on us. We crushed the *federales* on the plains of Oaxaca."

The two men shared a quiet reminiscent moment together, then El Guapo moved down the line.

Dusty was next. In a moment he and El Guapo would be eyeball to eyeball, nose to nose. Dusty scrooched down a little deeper into his serape, hoping it would muffle his face and forestall recognition.

"And you . . ." El Guapo broke off, stumped. Who was this *hombre*? Was this one of his men? He looked vaguely familiar, and El Guapo thought he knew most of them by sight. But his name . . .

"Uh . . .José," supplied Dusty.

"Jo SAY," echoed El Guapo heartily. "Of course, José. I knew that. Together, we —" We what?

"— burned the village . . ." prompted Dusty.

"Yes, burned the village and —"

"— raped the horses . . ."

"Raped the horses," echoed El Guapo. "And —"

"— rode off on the women . . ."

". . . rode off on the women . . . and we —"

"— plundered . . ."

"— plundered," agreed the bandit chief. "And —"

Now Dusty was stuck. What the hell did *bandidos* do besides plunder? He thought fast, an act to which he had yet to become accustomed.

"— pruned . . ." he said. It was the best he could come up with at such short notice.

"— pruned the —"

"— hedges . . ." supplied Dusty.

"— the hedges —"

". . . of many small villages," Dusty finished quickly, and let his breath out in relief.

"— of many small villages," El Guapo repeated. "WHO THE HELL ARE YOU?" he shrieked.

Jefe raced forward and yanked off Dusty's sombrero. "It's another one of the goddamn gringos," he reported. While two desperadoes took tight hold of Dusty's arms, Jefe spun him around and grabbed his six-guns out of their holsters. By a fortunate accident, they overlooked the knife that was tucked into the waistband of Dusty's trousers against the small of his back.

El Guapo exploded into wrath; he was terrible to see. Not only had the sanctity of his mountain stronghold been violated, but on his birthday, too! Where were the guards? Who was responsible for this outrage? Just wait until he got his hands on them! Heads were going to roll.

The German, meanwhile, was looking very hard at Dusty. There was something about this American, too, as well as that white-haired one they had captured earlier, that was very familiar. This one and the other one both. If only he could remember. . . . "Take this monkey away!"

yelled El Guapo. "Put him with that other *yanqui* imbecile! What is happening here today?" he demanded hotly. "Are gringos falling from the sky?"

No actor ever born could resist a cue like that. There was a ripping sound overhead as Ned Nederlander's spurs finally tore loose from the piñata, and Ned hurtled head-over-heels through the air and tumbled to the ground right at El Guapo's booted feet.

"*Sí*, chief, they are," Jefe answered the not-so-rhetorical question.

A savage smile of malevolent satisfaction spread over El Guapo's scruffy features. "Now we have *all* the Amigos," he purred evilly. Then his face darkened. "Today they all die. Take them away!"

Chapter Thirteen

"Vun moment, please!" thé German's voice rang out
with Teutonic harshness, commanding immediate silence.
"I know who zis man is!" He was pointing straight at
Ned.

There was a surprised grunt from El Guapo, a murmur
of astonishment racing through the crowd, and everybody's eyes turned to look at the tall, scarred man wearing
flying leathers.

"You do?" El Guapo's eyebrows shot up.

"Yes. It is Ned Nederlander." Now it was Ned's turn
to gasp. Who was this man? How did he know him?

The German marched toward Ned, who was being
roughly restrained by a pair of badmen, his arms pinned
behind his back.

"Who?" El Guapo was totally mystified. "Ned who?"

Now the German was facing Ned, his eyes boring into
the smaller man's face. "You are my favorite star of ze
silver screen," he told him.

"Really!" Ned almost exploded in relief.

"In Germany ze cinema is very popular. I have seen all your films. Including ven you vere known as Little Neddy Knickers."

Ned cast his eyes down in false modesty. "Well, that was a long time ago. . . ."

Now the German turned away and addressed the crowd at large. "It vas zis man who inspired me to learn ze art of ze qvick-draw. I looked up to zis man. I studied his every move. It vas my dream to be as fast as Ned Nederlander. I practiced every day for hours and hours. He vas a god to me!"

"A god! Well, I don't know about that," simpered Ned delightedly. "But it's always nice to meet a fan. . . ."

"But ven I heard about movie tricks," continued the German, his brow darkening under the leather helmet, "I vas crushed!"

"I never used trick photography!" denied Ned in a loud, indignant squeak. "Everything was always real!"

The German shook his head. "Zat is impossible," he answered flatly. "No vun is as fast as you appear to be."

"I *am* that fast," Ned insisted.

"Ve shall see."

"Happy to oblige," agreed Ned. "Does anyone have a watch? Preferably one with a second hand."

"I have a watch," volunteered El Guapo, eager to see what was going to happen.

But the German shook his head again with ominous emphasis. "No vatch. As you Americans say, ve play for keeps. Give him back his guns."

El Guapo grinned broadly and nodded his enthusiastic approval. This was exactly the kind of sadistic cat-and-mouse game he enjoyed the most. "Leave him here," he instructed his men, pointing at Dusty. "He might like to see his friend die."

Ned's eyes opened wide, and his mouth formed a horror-stricken "Oh" as he finally comprehended the full enormity of the situation. This German was challenging him to a duel! To the death! It was inconceivable.

What kind of man was this who could possibly want to kill Little Neddy Knickers?

Lucky Day almost had the hang of it now. There was a certain tempo to the turning of the wheel that he had become familiar with. Every nerve and muscle in his body was attuning itself to the rhythm of the ratchets, and all it took was every ounce of strength that he could muster. Sweat trickled down his face, and his jaws ached from gritting his teeth but he had managed to move himself forward in an odd, slow, stiff-legged manner, close to halfway across the room.

Sooner or later, he told himself, he was going to catch up with that winch. But it had better be sooner, because later might be too late. Those guards might be back any minute now, and then it would be all over for him.

Every once in a while he would make a misstep, and then the winch would turn in the opposite direction, causing Lucky to lose ground and fall back a few feet. Remember the old algebra problem of the frog in the well?

This frog falls down this well and has to keep hopping in an upward direction in order to get out. But for every few feet it hops out, it falls back a couple. How long will it take the frog to get out of its well — or Lucky to get out of his cell? Forward three feet, back one. Forward two, back one. What is the answer to the problem? For Lucky Day, the answer is possible death.

But he still didn't lose heart. Like a slave in the cotton fields or a deckhand on an old three-masted schooner, he had developed a kind of work chantey which he sang, or rather muttered, to himself in time with each movement of a cog.

"Gonna make it . . . gonna make it . . . gonna make it . . ." That was three steps forward.

Oops! There goes the winch, slipping in the wrong direction. "Never make it . . . never make it . . . never make it . . ." That was three steps back.

Yet, little by little, inch by painful inch, the "gonna make its" began to outnumber the "never make its." Closer he came, always closer to the winch and the dangling set of precious keys. Just one more step, Lucky! Great, attaboy, now just one more. . . .

"MADE IT," yelled Lucky triumphantly, reaching the winch and hanging on for dear life. "I made it!"

Way to go, Lucky! Now all you have to do is pull the pin that holds the spring. . . . Pull the pin, Lucky! No, don't let go, don't relax, not even for an instant! . . . Oh, no! I can't look!

Too late. In that nanosecond in which the exhausted Lucky allowed his aching muscles to relax, the spring, which was wound up fully to its tightest, sproinged again. The winch spun around like a ship's wheel with nobody at the helm, and Lucky Day went zipping through the air, pulled at top speed by his chains and slamming up against the far wall like a fly smashed by a giant swatter.

A horrified Ned Nederlander could not believe that this was actually happening to him. El Guapo's *bandidos* had actually cleared a path for him and the German, a long, lonely corridor down which the pair of them now stood facing each other, one at each end. The badmen were grinning and laughing and poking one another in delight over the show they were about to witness. No, it couldn't be true! It was a scene from a western, any western, the scene they call "The Mexican Standoff." How ironic that it should be happening to Ned in real life and right here in Mexico! Sometimes life imitates art just a tad too close for comfort.

One of the *bandidos* had stripped off his own gunbelt and had given it over to Jefe, who was handing the belt and the loaded guns to Ned. But Ned shook his head and put up one hand, refusing them.

"You don't understand," he protested vehemently. "I don't shoot at people. It's against my upbringing. Call it etiquette, consideration for others, whatever . . . but no!"

This declaration elicited coarse guffaws from the *bandidos* and a fierce scowl from the German. The German had been fondling the pearl-inlaid butts of his own pistols lovingly; now he drew his guns from their holsters. The dueling scar on his cruel face stood out red with anticipation against the pastiness of his skin.

Cocking the six-shooters, the German whirled and fired. Two piñatas burst open overhead, spilling their birthday presents onto the ground. Oh, he was fast on the draw all right, very fast.

The German grinned a terrifying grin. In a moment or two, Ned Nederlander's guts would be spilling out on the ground, just like those *idiotisch* papier-mâché toys.

"I have vaited years for zis moment," he exulted. "Und now it has arrived."

Ned turned pale, and his stomach began to churn. How he wished that he was anyplace else but here! He glanced over at Dusty, who was being held captive by two large and burly desperadoes. The two Amigos locked eyes for an instant, saying a silent farewell. They both allowed their thoughts to turn briefly and fondly to the third Amigo, Lucky Day, who by now must have gone to that big film studio in the sky. . . .

Well, not quite gone, but almost. Lucky was still locked into a titanic struggle with that damn winch, which had just pulled an ace out of its mechanical sleeve. The chains had fouled a little with all that unaccustomed heavy to-ing and fro-ing; they no longer fit perfectly and precisely on the ratchets. The result was that, if they worked Lucky could, with incredible effort, schlepp himself forward. But if they didn't, an arm or a leg would be yanked up suddenly into the air, and Lucky Day would dangle there like an oversize marionette on iron strings.

Whenever Lucky won, he went forward a step. Whenever the winch won, Lucky did his Pinocchio impression. Take a step, right arm goes up, take another step, left leg goes up. And so on, for what seemed to Lucky to be an eternity.

The only thing that kept him going was the thought that Dusty and Ned might still be alive. If so, they'd be needing him badly. How could there be Three Amigos when there were only two?

He continued to strain while the sweat streamed off his brow in salty rivulets, running down into the collar of his ruffled shirt. At last, incredibly, just as the last ounce of strength was ebbing from his body, Lucky reached the winch, grabbed hold of it, held on tight, and pulled out the pin.

The device was disarmed. The taut spring was released, but this time it didn't take the chains with it. He had done it. Gasping and trembling with relief, Lucky reached for the keys, unlocked his arms and legs, and then the barred door of the cell. Lucky Day was free!

"What kind of guns are these?" Ned squeaked nervously, eyeballing the huge *pistolas* that Jefe was holding out to him.

The bandit second in command uttered a raucous guffaw. "These are *men's* guns, gringo. Not like them sissy little guns you like!"

"Enough!" barked the German. "Put on guns, *und mach schnell*! Let's go, Nederlander!"

With the greatest reluctance, Ned accepted the gunbelt. The weight of it surprised him; the guns were so heavy he had trouble strapping them on around his waist. For years he had been accustomed to his own six-shooters; they had been custom-made to his size and the contours of his hands; the sights were perfectly aligned, the grips perfectly balanced.

Ned knew all their perfections and all their imperfections; every foible of those guns was imprinted on his memory. How on earth was he going to outdraw a marksman like the German with a pair of strange guns he couldn't even lift, let alone shoot? But there was no way out. It was all over for him. The end of Ned Nederlander, the finish of Little Neddy Knickers. He was doomed. There went The Three Amigos.

The bandits had paced off the distance; twenty paces now remained between the German and Ned. An icy smile played grimly about the German's stony lips, and his hands hovered in the air just over the handles of his guns, ready to draw. He had been looking forward to this for a lifetime; it wasn't given to every man to meet up with his idol and shoot him dead.

As for Ned, he had never been so frightened in his life. His mouth was dry, and his knees were knocking together so hard he thought everybody could hear them. The palms of his hands were wet and slippery, and would probably slide right off the gun butts. He was sweating profusely.

The German, on the other hand, was as dry as the desert air, only cooler. But his hands had dropped almost imperceptibly lower, almost touching the revolvers now. And then, with lightning speed, so fast that if you blinked you'd miss it, the German drew his guns and pointed them at Ned.

The cracking sound of two shots split the air, and the German reeled back, wounded. The unbelievable had come to pass. As fast as the German was, Ned Nederlander was faster still! Even handicapped by the strange, heavy, clumsy guns, Ned had drawn and fired before the other man's hands could tighten on the triggers! So much for trick photography!

But the recoil from the heavy *pistolas* sent little Ned sailing backward through the air, the six-guns flying out of his hands. One of them fell to the ground at his feet, but the other gun rose in a high trajectory, high . . . high . . . away. . . .

A hand reached out to seize it. Lucky Day's hand.

As he grabbed the gun butt, Lucky saw the German's two companions swing into immediate action, pulling their pistols from their leather holsters and aiming them at Ned.

Things moved so quickly now that time and events simply blurred, like film shot out of focus at the wrong speed. Lucky fired a shot, wounding one of the Germans, while Dusty, in one strong movement, pulled loose from his captors, reached behind him, and drew the knife from the waistband of his trousers. He threw. The knife sliced cleanly through the air, pinning the other German to the wall. Three down, a hundred to go.

"Aaarrrrgghhhh!" yelled El Guapo, enraged beyond measure. He grabbed his weapon and aimed it at Ned, his finger reaching for the trigger.

"I've had enough of these gringos!" he shouted. "*Vaya con Dios*, Amigo!"

But before he could fire, a voice called to him from the balcony above. "Not so fast, El Guapo. I'll fill you so full of lead you'll be using your dick for a pencil!"

The bandit chief looked up. Lucky Day was standing there smiling, with a large *pistola* aimed straight at El Guapo's heart.

"What do you mean?" El Guapo called up to Lucky.

Jefe was so used to being the target of the boss's questions that he quavered, "I don't know" in reply.

"You shut up!"

"So you thought you could outsmart The Three Amigos!" laughed Lucky. "Well, not this time. You have met your match! Ned, cover El Guapo!"

Quickly, Ned Nederlander retrieved the gun from the ground and pointed it against the bandit leader's head. With El Guapo covered, it was easy for Dusty Bottoms to take a pistol from the gunbelt of the nearest bandit. He almost dropped it, but managed to hang on to it, juggling it by the barrel until he could get his hands on the grip.

"Now throw down your guns," commanded Lucky.

The badmen hesitated, and Ned pressed his gun more tightly against El Guapo's head.

"Do as he says," conceded El Guapo angrily.

There was a clatter of weapons hitting the ground.

"Not you, Dusty," said Lucky from the balcony.

"Oh, sorry."

"Now, everybody lie down and put your hands behind your head. Good. Not you, Dusty."

"Oh, sorry."

"All right, Ned, open the gates."

Ned Nederlander backed to the gates, taking El Guapo with him, his weapon still pressing hard on the bandit's temple. It was only the fact that their leader was being held at gunpoint that kept a hundred men at bay. His gun drawn to cover them both, Dusty came up to Ned. In a split second, Lucky was down from the balcony and had joined the other two. Ned pushed back the heavy wooden bolt that barred the gate; the gates swung open and there was Carmen Sanchez, sitting astride a pretty pinto and holding the reins of three swift horses.

The Three Amigos mounted up and tugged at the reins. The horses wheeled, prancing in the air and snorting, ready for anything.

"Now, don't you dare pick up those guns and try to follow us!" Ned warned the bandits as the four of them rode away, leaving the bandits still lying on the ground with their hands behind their heads.

"After them!" yelled El Guapo furiously. "Kill them! I want them dead! *A los caballos, muchachos!* To the horses!"

One of the women brought him his bandoliers of cart-ridges, and El Guapo strapped them on over his party suit, jamming his guns into their holsters. Now it was no more Señor Nice Guy. Now that he was dressed in his badman outfit, once again in command, was he ever thirsty for blood!

At El Guapo's barked orders, the desperadoes immediately scrambled to their feet and scrabbled around for their weapons. Then about thirty-five of them ran for the horses and rode out of the gate full gallop behind El Guapo. The party was over. The disappointed girls waved bye-bye, and one of them called after him in a forlorn voice, "El Guapo! You forgot your sweater!"

The Three Amigos and Carmen rode straight for the open field that lay ahead of them. Behind them they could hear the thunder of hoofbeats as the bandidos gave chase. Dusty cast a despairing glance over his shoulder.

"We'll never make it! They're gaining on us!"

But Ned's mouth was set, Ned's face was determined. "I know what to do. Stay with me."

"Now we have them!" gloated El Guapo. "There they go, into that open field." Cruelly, he spurred his horse with a vicious kick in the ribs, picking up speed. The bandit horde followed his lead, riding hell-for-leather after The Three Amigos plus one.

The distance between the two groups is closing fast. Soon the vicious killers will have caught up with our heroes.

The red biplane was standing in the field exactly where the German had landed. Talk about state of the art! What a beauty she was! With a 110-horsepower Le Rhone rotary engine, a range of 130 miles, a climbing speed of 720 feet a minute, the canvas-fuselaged single-engine aeroplane could attain a maximum speed of an incredible 103 miles an hour!

"What luck! It's the Tubbman 601," cried Lucky. "You can fly one, Ned." He chuckled with relief.

"Well, not exactly." Ned was looking somewhat embarrassed, and seemed to be having trouble meeting the other Amigos' eyes.

"But you said you flew one in *Little Neddy Goes to War*," Dusty pointed out, confused.

"Actually, my stunt man did."

"You bastard!" howled Lucky, and raised his hand to hit him.

"But I think I kind of remember. . . ." added Ned softly.

"Remember or not, you'd better hurry," said Dusty. "Here comes El Guapo and about a thousand of his men."

The four of them scrambled off their horses and climbed up into the two-seater airship, Ned at the controls in the cockpit, Carmen, Lucky, and Dusty crammed tightly into the passenger seat behind. The Tubbman had no roof or canopy; the seats were wide open to the elements.

"Hmmmmmm, let me see," murmured Ned half to himself. "What do all those dials and needles mean? This handle seems to turn this way . . . no, that way. And this thingamajig over here, that's got to be the control for . . ."

"For God's sake, get a move on!" urged Lucky impatiently. "We're staring death in the face here!"

"Hold your horses," called Ned over his shoulder. "If a thing is worth doing, it's worth doing well. Besides, we may be overloaded. I'm not sure this thing can get off the ground with four of us."

"There they are! Seize them! Shoot them! Kill them!" hollered El Guapo, red in the face. "At least catch them before they get away!"

But it was already too late. The Tubbman 601 was lumbering down the field straight at them, her wheels rolling, nose lifting, engine coughing, propeller turning, the canvas-covered wings straining.

The bandits were forced to scatter out of the airship's path or be mowed down like so many bowling pins. The plane rolled right on through them, but every time Ned tried to take off, the Tubbman, overloaded, refused. They kept making little abortive hops, like a big red rabbit.

"Regroup!" screamed El Guapo over the noise of the

engine. "They'll never make it! After them, *muchachos*, after them! Shoot!" He took off after the plane at top speed, his men following close behind.

As soon as they were within rifle range, the bandits began to fire. Bullets whizzed through the air around the Tubbman's ears, one or two of them hitting the fuselage. If the wings should be damaged, they might tear off in flight! Frantically, Ned Nederlander hit switches, turned dials, pressed buttons, pulled back on the joystick.

At last, just when it appeared to be most hopeless, just when the *bandidos* were catching up with them, a miracle occurred. With a mighty roaring noise that split the heavens, the aeroplane was aloft! In the air! Flying! How about that! Isn't that Ned the cat's pajamas?

"So long, El Guapo!" laughed Lucky Day as the Tubbman buzzed the bandit, dipping her wings once as she started her climb into the wild blue yonder.

"So long, my ass! I'll see you in Santo Poco!" yelled the furious bandit, emptying his revolver at the plane but missing every shot.

I'll see you in Santo Poco. It was no idle threat. His men, catching up with El Guapo, reined their horses in and turned to the south, riding hard, their brand-new and deadly efficient rifles loaded and ready to kill.

Chapter Fourteen

With Ned Nederlander as pilot and Carmen Sanchez as navigator, the Tubbman 601 chugged its way southward to the village of Santo Poco. Because she was carrying an extra passenger, the biplane couldn't gain much altitude, so they could see every detail of the terrain. Mountains and desert unfolded beneath them like a living geodesic-survey map. They could see the smallest detail, even the horns on the skinny stray cows. Carmen's eyes were round with wonder. Only a couple of days ago, she hadn't known that aeroplanes even existed; today she was riding in one, actually flying through the air. Was this world not a marvelous place indeed?

"There! Look!" she cried, pointing over the side. "There's Santo Poco! It has to be! There is no church!"

They all looked down. Carmen was right. The three Amigos could clearly see the villagers working down below — picking up rubble, clearing away debris, nailing up new doors, making bricks of adobe mud to rebuild their town.

At the noise of the engine, the villagers dropped their tools and looked up in amazement. A big red bird with double wings was coming down out of the sky! Carrying people! It was a miracle!

Ned pushed forward on the joystick, and the Tubbman's nose dipped. He began to circle slowly for a landing, looking for a likely spot in the desert which surrounded the village. Carmen pointed one out, and Ned steered straight for it. He was getting the hang of it now. The biplane made a neat three-point landing just outside the village, bounced up, hit the ground a little harder, bounced up again, and continued its bouncing and rolling, its rising and falling, until it bounced right into the village, down the main street and came sharply to a stop, both wings breaking off.

The astonished Santo Pocanos could not believe their eyes. They came running on the double to witness this marvel more closely. Chattering excitedly to one another, they gathered around the Tubbman.

Carmen Sanchez climbed shakily out on the broken wing and addressed the crowd. "El Guapo is on his way! He will be here by tomorrow!"

A gasp of horror arose from the people, and many of the women crossed themselves in fear. Papa Sanchez, *Mamacita*, and Rodrigo rushed forward to hug and kiss Carmen, whom they had never expected to see alive again. As for the others, all they could think about was the girl's warning. El Guapo was coming! they told one another, terrified. This time he would put an end to Santo Poco for sure! He and his bandits would steal everything he could lay his hands on, and then murder them all! *Madre de Dios!*

Now a smiling, waving Lucky Day stepped out of the biplane and joined Carmen on the broken wing, using it as a podium to address the crowd of villagers.

If The Three Amigos hadn't brought Carmen Sanchez back home safe and sound, Santo Poco would have attacked them with fists, brooms and broken pieces of pottery from the water jars that El Guapo had shot to shards. But her very presence among them was living testimony that Lucky, Dusty, and Ned might not actually be the total cowards and screw-ups they appeared to be, so even the most doubtful of the villagers was willing to pay at least *some* attention to Lucky's words.

"Someday the people of Santo Poco will have to face El Guapo. You might as well do it now!" began Lucky.

There was a general shaking of heads and murmurs of disagreement, but still the villagers remained tuned in.

"In a way," continued Lucky earnestly, "all of us have an El Guapo that we have to face someday. For some, shyness might be their El Guapo. For others, lack of confidence might be their El Guapo. For us, El Guapo is a big, dangerous guy who wants to kill us. But as sure as I'm sitting on this horse, the people of Santo Poco can conquer their own personal El Guapo, who also happens to be the real El Guapo."

"He's brilliant," breathed Dusty Bottoms, awed. The nicest thing about Dusty was that he left thinking to those whose job it was to think.

The people of Santo Poco scratched their heads and looked at one another, completely puzzled. Sitting on what horse? But they did glean the kernel of what Lucky Day was telling them — that they were supposed to face up to the *bandidos* and fight for Santo Poco.

"But how can our small village defend itself against so many?" asked Papa Sanchez.

Now it was Ned Nederlander's turn to inspire them. "By using the skill and talents of the people of Santo Poco!" he said, his eyes shining with encouragement. "This is not a town of weaklings! We will turn your skills against El Guapo. Now, what is it that this town really does well?"

There was a moment of blank silence, then Carlos spoke

up. "We can sew," he offered. "Santo Poco is famous for its beautiful serapes."

"Sewing!" cried Dusty. "There you go! If only we'd known that earlier!" But his brow was furrowed. Sewing?

Lucky Day, however, was deep in thought. Sewing . . . sewing. . . .

Ned, Dusty, do you remember our film *Amigos, Amigos, Amigos*?"

Dusty's nose wrinkled up in distaste. "Quiet, someone might hear you," he said, proving that he remembered it all too well.

"Remember what we did in that picture?" Lucky asked significantly.

Dusty racked his brains, but Ned had already caught on, and his little face was suddenly alight, "Jeez, do you think it could work?" he breathed.

Lucky's chin shot up, and that old Amigos confidence and leadership positively radiated from his every pore. He turned his face so that Dusty and Ned could see his profile.

"It's *got* to work! It's our only hope." He turned to the villagers. "Okay, listen up, everybody. Gather around. Here's what I want you to do. . . ."

As the people of Santo Poco crowded around to hear Lucky Day's idea, their peasant faces revealed their changing reactions, expressing 1) stubborn opposition, then 2) ridicule, then 3) doubt, next 4) a dawning hope, and, finally, 5) determination. Lucky had won them over. Come what may, come El Guapo and his men, come defeat, disaster, death, and the six o'clock news, The Three Amigos had won their confidence and trust. Santo Poco was committed.

They set to work immediately, every man and woman to his or her job, as the Three Amigos showed them exactly what to do. Even the children helped out, threading the bobbins for the sewing machines, running back and forth on their sturdy young legs, their arms filled with more supplies. The humming sound of the foot-pedal Singers could be heard all over the village at every moment of the day. As soon as one team of sewers was forced to quit because of exhaustion, another sprang forward to take its place at the machines.

"Sew!" exhorted Lucky, running from place to place to supervise and encourage. "Sew for your lives!"

They sewed. Far into the night Santo Poco sewed by the wavery light of oil-filled kerosene lamps. They sewed until they were ready to drop, and then they sewed some more.

Meanwhile, Lucky, Dusty, and Ned were getting other things ready. If Lucky's idea worked, El Guapo and his men were in for one big surprise. *If* Lucky's idea worked. . . .

The church itself had been demolished, dynamited by El Guapo's *bandidos*, but the people of Santo Poco had saved the bell. For many years it had rung every morning to awaken the townsfolk, and this morning it rang longer and more loudly than ever.

But nobody was there to hear it, not by the looks of things. The town appeared completely empty — not one dog barked, not one baby cried. There was no welcome sound of pots and pans banging on the stove, no smell of refried beans or boiling coffee. No smoke arose from the village chimneys that were still standing. Except for The Three Amigos, there seemed to be nobody left in Santo Poco.

The Three Amigos had not slept, but they were not tired. Exhilaration and hope gave them all the energy they required. They were needed here; they were doing something for the people of this village, and that feeling was more invigorating, more uplifting than any they had ever gotten from their names in lights, their faces on billboards, their Hollywood mansion, their fancy custom-made clothes, their chauffeur-driven limousines, or even their autograph hounds. This was what real heroism was all about. This was not the silver screen, this was *life*!

In their bedroom in the Sanchez household, The Three Amigos were getting ready. Their outfits had been lovingly sponged clean and pressed by Carmen and Rosita. The silver bullion on their Amigos suits was polished until it shone; their boots were buffed and their ruffles were fluffed. Despite the wear and tear and trauma they'd been through, the costumes looked fantastic, as fresh as when they'd stolen them from the studio.

Carefully, almost ritualistically, Lucky, Dusty, and Ned donned their Three Amigos suits and strapped on their six-shooters. Lucky tested his rope to make sure there were no knots in it; Dusty put a new sharp edge on his trusty knife.

"I hope this plan works, Lucky," said Ned Nederlander.

"I hope so, too, Ned," replied Lucky Day.

"I hope so, too," chimed in Dusty Bottoms.

"Me, too," said Ned.

"Me, too," Lucky said.

"I really hope so," added Dusty.

"Let's just say it had *better* work," and Lucky scowled a little.

"Yeah." Ned nodded his head. "It had better."

"Yeah," agreed Dusty. "It really better work."

They were ready. "Let's get goin'," said Lucky, wasting no words.

"Yes, let's," said Ned.

But there was an anxious look on Dusty Bottoms' face. "Lucky, I just remembered something," he said slowly.

"Yes?"

"It didn't work in the movie."

"El Guapo, we have been riding for hours. The horses are tired and the men could use a rest. Can't we stop for just a little while?" Jefe looked imploringly at the bandit chieftain.

"There will be no stopping! Besides, we will soon be there! I want that girl back; she is my property. I stole her fair and square!"

El Guapo's eyes were red-rimmed and trail dust covered his sombrero and his stubbly whiskers like a fine cloud, but he sat tall in the saddle and stared grimly ahead, to where Santo Poco lay at the edge of the desert. "And I want those three damn Amigos dead, do you hear me, Jefe? Dead, all of them — one, two, three!"

"I hear you, El Guapo."

Silently, purposefully, the bandits rode on.

It was almost time. By Lucky's calculations, El Guapo and his men should be here within the hour. Alone, The Three Amigos strode shoulder to shoulder through the empty streets to the center of the deserted square; alone, Lucky, Dusty, and Ned checked their weapons, mounted their horses, and rode slowly to the edge of town, to the place where the desert met the irrigated cornfields. From this way the *bandidos* would be coming.

In that stopping place they sat, waiting for the showdown, their eyes shadowed by their gigantic sombreros, silent, each man lost in his thoughts. Yet each man's thoughts were much the same as those of the other two.

How much they had changed in only a few short days, these Three Amigos! How little they had known of truth and justice, of courage and standing up for one's beliefs, of fighting for one's rights, of the moral and unending struggle between good and evil.

All they used to think of was their billing and their box office. They had arrived in Mexico three shallow, vain, out-of-work actors and now . . . Well, let others tell their story, let those who are better qualified to do so narrate how The Three Amigos stood up to the notorious El Guapo and his thirty-five . . . no, fifty . . . no, make that two hundred men!

Let others tell their story, for how could they be sure that they would live to tell it themselves? But, thought each of them, if they *did* live to tell the story, what a hell of a movie it would make!

In the distance, a telltale cloud of desert dust. From

the distance, the sound of many pounding hooves. El Guapo. It was time.

Very soon it will all be over, for better or for worse, for life or for death. Very soon The Three Amigos will be testing for real this plan of Lucky Day's, this plan that didn't work in *Amigos, Amigos, Amigos,* a film that also didn't work.

At the head of the riders, El Guapo put up his hand, signaling "halt." The band of cutthroat desperados came to a stop several hundred yards outside the village. Something was ahead of him, blocking his way; three somethings, in fact.

Side by side, The Three Amigos rode out slowly to meet the gang. In less than a minute, they were face to face, three men against thirty-five. Rifle bolts clicked ominously, triggers waiting only for a sign from their leader.

"Where is the girl?" demanded El Guapo. His own trigger finger was itching him like blazes; he wanted to grab his guns and shoot those three gringos right out of the saddle, just blow them away.

"You can't have the girl," answered Ned Nederlander quietly. "And if you ride into town, you will have to deal with the three of us."

El Guapo rose in his stirrups and turned around to his men. "You hear that?" he laughed sarcastically. "If we ride into town we will have to deal with the three of them!"

The tickled bandits pounded their fists on their pommels and laughed until the tears came to their wicked eyes. Some of them even went so far as to make rude, mocking, animalistic noises, such as pretending to belch or break wind. Badmen can be so coarse.

But Ned's expression did not change; it remained one of calm dignity and courage. "Sometimes three can fight like fifty if their cause is just. We will no longer allow you to treat these people like dirt beneath your feet."

Another deep belly laugh from El Guapo, a laugh tinged with scorn and contempt. "The people? The people? Do you think they will help you? They are like sheep! They run at the first sign of danger."

"El Guapo," said Ned quite firmly, "if you enter this village, you will never leave it alive!"

This speech occasioned a burst of mean-spirited hilarity and a lot of nasty remarks and some finger pointing.

"All right," nodded Ned quietly. "We'll be waiting." The bandits' mocking laughter followed The Three Amigos as they turned and rode away, back into Santo Poco. They didn't see Jefe raise his rifle and aim at Ned's back; they didn't see El Guapo scowl and pull the rifle barrel down before his aide could fire.

"When the time comes, Jefe, these three are mine! Do you understand me? *Mine!*"

"Boy," remarked Dusty happily as they cantered, "we haven't gotten laughs like that in a long time."

But the time for laughter and good times was over; it was the hour for attack — for the burning and shooting and the raping and looting. El Guapo's men have ridden far and fast; they are eager to get on with it. It's time to take care of business.

The rifles were cocked now, and the bandits were ready. El Guapo wheeled his horse around and shouted after The Three Amigos, "Hey, you Amigos. . ."

But they were gone, out of sight. Only his own voice came back to him, echoing out the desert. Nothing stirred in Santo Poco. And no sign at all of The Three Amigos.

"*Adiós, Amigos!*" growled the *bandido*. Then, to his men, "*Vamanos, muchachos.*" Let's go, boys. El Guapo pressed his knees hard into Maricón's flanks, kneeing the horse forward. His men followed. Into the little farming village of Santo Poco they rode with bullets in their rifles and murder in their hearts.

At the center of the village, in the middle of the town square, they came to a stop. Where was everybody? Not even a chicken or a stray mutt to be seen. Did an entire village just pick up and run away?

"Where are you, my friends?" called El Guapo slyly, the fox calling to the hens.

Suddenly he had an answer. There came the sharp crack of gunfire and the whiz of bullets, and several *bandidos* clutched at their chests and pitched out of their saddles and into the dusty plaza.

And there, over there, standing on a rooftop, The Three Amigos, each of them with a pair of deadly six-guns in his hands, letting fly a hail of bullets.

"There they are, El Guapo!" yelled Jefe, taking aim.

At Jefe's cry, the bandits whirled and fired wildly at the place where The Three Amigos had been standing.

But there they weren't. They had disappeared from view. No, look! Suddenly, as if by magic, there they were again, firing down at the gang from a rooftop *across the square!* How the hell did they get over there so fast?

"Now they are over there, El Guapo!" hollered Jefe, and once again the bandits opened fire. But once again their targets had vanished off the face of the earth. It was spooky as hell; the *bandidos* weren't too crazy about this turn of events. With this last salvo from the Amigos' blazing six-shooters, they had lost at least five more men.

Without warning, a door to one of the little adobe houses burst open and The Three Amigos rushed across the village square, firing as they went. Several more of El Guapo's *bandidos* bit the dust and died cursing, but before a single bandit could squeeze off a shot, the heroic trio had run through another doorway and were safely out of range.

"They went in through that door!" called El Guapo. "Get them!"

Five *bandidos*, rifles cocked, ran for the doorway. But before they could reach it, The Three Amigos popped up from behind a wagon which was parked at the curb and mowed the five down in a rain of bullets.

What the hell was going on here? The carnage was getting to be frightful, but so far it was only the bad guys who'd suffered any losses. The Amigos were as yet unscathed. This was too much for some of the *bandidos*.

"El Guapo! They are everywhere!" At least a dozen men threw down their rifles and ran for their horses without a backward look, heedless of their leader's angry shouts after them.

"Come back, you cowards! Come back and fight! These are men, and they can die like men! They are not ghosts!"

Weren't they? Then how come The Three Amigos were seen *here*, and a second later, they appeared *there*? The situation was getting to El Guapo, who fired at . . . nothing, turned again and shot . . . nobody. But he had just seen them! They appeared in an instant, and the very next instant disappeared, but The three Amigos' smoking guns kept taking their toll of the villains.

All around him, El Guapo's men were either dropping like flies or turning tail and running off.

From the corner of his eye the bandit boss saw Jefe scramble on his horse and ride off, but before he could yell after him what he thought of such cowardice and treachery, before he could tell his second in command that he, El Guapo the brave, vowed never to wear that birthday sweater again, it was too late. For El Guapo the game was over.

He caught the big one, a bullet in the chest. El Guapo bought the farm, chickens, pigs, and all. He spun around, staggering, his eyes bulging from their sockets with shock and indignation.

Hey, this is me, El Guapo! How is this possible? El Guapo doesn't die! I guess this just isn't my day!

When they saw their leader stagger and fall, saw the blood spreading crimson through his serape, the *bandidos* — what few were left, between the dead and the fleeing — threw in the towel. There was no future in this gunfight, they shrugged as they ran for their lives. Here was the perfect opportunity for a midlife career change.

It was over. The battle was won. The streets of Santo

Poco were littered with dead and dying desperados, and never again would any gang of marauding bandits dare to make free with the people of this little farming village. Future generations of bandits would hold their *niños* on their knees and tell them of the terrible exploits of The Three Amigos, three men who laughed at death, and the *bandidos* would say, "And remember, when you grow up, stay the hell out of Santo Poco!"

El Guapo lay breathing his next-to-last, his gun still in his hand, his head propped up by the water trough. Lucky, Dusty, and Ned walked quietly over to him.

The breath rattled and rasped in the *bandido*'s chest; he tried to speak, but no more than a whisper escaped his dying lips. Lucky Day bent closer to hear El Guapo's words.

"How did you do it?" the dying man asked. "I never saw such fighting. You were everywhere." He coughed, and a trickle of blood came out of the side of his mouth. "The great El Guapo is no more," he wheezed. "Defeated by only three men."

"Well, not exactly three, El Guapo," smiled Lucky, and then he beckoned.

El Guapo's vision was blurred; he was sinking fast. Was this a delusion? Three Amigos were coming out of the house toward him. And over there, three more, all identically dressed in those flamboyant getups. And three more, and three more, and three more . . . The whole damn town of Santo Poco was dressed up as The Three Amigos!

"More like a hundred and thirty-three," said Lucky proudly.

El Guapo grimaced, partly in pain and partly because he'd been so thoroughly taken. "Oh, that was some good trick," he rasped. "Come closer, I have something to tell you."

Lucky Day leaned in closer to hear.

El Guapo raised his gun hand feebly and shot Lucky in the foot. "That was a good trick, too," chuckled the bandit, and croaked.

Chapter Fifteen

So what is there left to say? The thrilling part of the story is over; this part is only happiness, good times, and good feelings. No more danger, and we've run out of villains, no more derring-do for the daring trio to do, just a bunch of grateful villagers and three very tired but very happy, very fulfilled Amigos.

For now The Three Amigos are heroes indeed. They can see it in the faces of the people of Santo Poco, who now regard them with respect and admiration, who hasten to give them tortillas and bouquets of flowers, or throw rose petals in the paths of their horses. They can see it in the prideful face of young Rodrigo Sanchez, for wasn't he one of their very first believers, and wasn't it he who had helped to bring The Three Amigos to Santo Poco?

They can see it in the lovely countenance and shining eyes of Carmen Sanchez, whose idea it had been in the first place to bring them all the way from Hollywood. They hadn't let her down.

But most of all, they could feel it in themselves — a new pride, a new sense of self-worth, a new confidence in a job well-done. Lucky, Dusty, and Ned had been put to the test, they had been tested as it's given to very few to be tested, and they had come through with flying colors. They had earned the right to wear their ridiculous outfits and call themselves The Three Amigos.

Now it was time to say good-bye, time for Lucky Day, Dusty Bottoms, and Ned Nederlander to mosey along into the future. A celebrating crowd of relieved and rejoicing villagers pressed around them to wish them Godspeed, which made it rather tricky going for the horses.

Papa Sanchez came running up wordlessly to squeeze their hands in gratitude, for he didn't trust himself to speak, so large was the lump in his throat. Then he rushed off into his casa. *Mamacita*, sobbing openly and happily, threw her arms around their necks, one Amigo at a time. But young Rodrigo wasn't able to part with them so easily.

The boy ran up to Ned, clutching at his stirrups, tears coursing down his youthful cheeks. "I want to go with you! I want to go with you!"

Ned leaned down from his saddle and touched the weeping boy lightly on his thick black hair.

"No, Rodrigo," he told him gently and with sympathy, "there is still much to be done here. Your village needs you, and your family needs you. We are men without homes; we were meant to wander."

"You will always have a home with us here in Santo Poco, Señor Ned," sobbed the boy.

"Thank you, Rodrigo."

Then Rosita, Carmen's friend, emerged from the crowd, pushing her way closer to The Three Amigos. "Will you come back to Santo Poco?" she asked huskily.

"When our work is done here, we will return," promised Lucky with noble gravity.

"What work?" asked Dusty. As usual, he was three beats behind the rest of the world.

"I will be waiting," the girl said smokily, and grabbing

Dusty Bottoms by the ears, she planted a big, wet, sexy tongue kiss right smack on his astonished but not unwilling mouth.

"I will be waiting, too," said Carmen Sanchez. Slowly, gracefully, she came toward The Three Amigos, her eyes smoldering with hidden fires, yet at the same time glistening with unshed tears.

Hot damn! At last! Lucky Day grinned, closed his eyes, and puckered up. But nothing happened. He opened his eyes to see Carmen already involved in a long, torrid, and soulful kiss — with Ned Nederlander. Ned? Little Neddy Knickers?

Now Papa Sanchez was emerging from his house. In his hands was a heavy cloth bag, tied at the neck. It clinked and jingled when he walked. Carrying it over to The Three Amigos, he held it up with some difficulty.

"You have done what you said you would do," he told them. "Long will the memory of The Three Amigos live in the hearts of the people of Santo Poco. We are proud to give you all we have. . . ." And he offered them the clinking sack.

"Here, I'll take that." Ned Nederlander reached down from his saddle and took the sack, hefting it with appreciation. He looked at his buddies. The Three Amigos exchanged glances and grins, then Ned gallantly tossed the bag of gold back to the villager.

"Our reward is that justice has been done!" cried Ned. Papa Sanchez's knees buckled under the impact.

"Adiós, my friends!" said Lucky, beginning his farewell remarks.

"You were right, Carmen. They did not take it," said her father.

The girl looked at him with puzzled eyes. "Papa, where did that gold come from?" she whispered. "I thought this village had no money!"

Her father looked a little uncomfortable and didn't meet her gaze. "Well, it wasn't exactly gold —"

"Papa! What was in that sack?"

"About twenty-five pesos."

"But it was so heavy! And it jingled. Papa! Look at me! What was in that sack?!"

"Well, you know that pile of old horseshoes out behind the corral . . ."

"*Papa!*"

"And remember," continued Lucky Day, "wherever there is injustice you will find us —"

"Wherever there is suffering, we'll be there —" added Dusty Bottoms.

"Wherever liberty is threatened," rang out Ned Nederlander's clear voice, "you will find —"

"THE THREE AMIGOS!" they chorused.

Lucky, Dusty, and Ned took off their sombreros and waved them to the cheering crowd. Then, putting them back on, they tugged at their horses' reins, making their gallant steeds rear upward, their hooves paw bravely at the sky. As one they executed perfectly the famous Three Amigos salute — one, two: hands crossed on chest; three: hands on hips. And they rode off, shoulder to shoulder, into the setting sun, going in search of their next adventure. And you know they'll find it.

Adios, amigos.

HERE IS YOUR CHANCE TO ORDER SOME OF OUR BEST

HISTORICAL ROMANCES

BY SOME OF YOUR FAVORITE AUTHORS

____ **DARK WINDS** — Virginia Coffman
Their fiery passion unleashed a tempest of . . . DARK
WINDS   7701-0405-3/$3.95

____ **KISS OF GOLD** — Samantha Harte
First he taught her to live . . . then he taught her to love.
7701-0529-7/$3.50

____ **MISTRESS OF MOON HILL** — Jill Downie
From the ashes of her heart, he kindled a new flame.
7701-0424-X/$3.95

____ **SWEET WHISPERS** — Samantha Harte
She struggled with her dark past in the hope of a new love.
7701-0496-7/$3.50

____ **THE WIND & THE SEA** — Marsha Canham
Passion and intrigue on the high seas. 7701-0415-0/$3.95

Prices subject to change without notice

- -

BOOKS BY MAIL

 320 Steelcase Rd. E.
Markham, Ont., L3R 2M1

In the U.S. -
210 5th Ave., 7th Floor
New York, N.Y. 10010

Please send me the books I have checked above. I am enclos-
ing a total of $_____ (Please add 1.00 for one book and
50 cents for each additional book.) My cheque or money order
is enclosed. (No cash or C.O.D.'s please.)

Name _____
Address _____ Apt. _____
City _____
Prov./State _____ P.C./Zip _____

(HIS/ROM)

FREE!!
BOOKS BY MAIL
CATALOGUE

BOOKS BY MAIL will share with you our current bestselling books as well as hard to find specialty titles in areas that will match your interests. You will be updated on what's new in books at no cost to you. Just fill in the coupon below and discover the convenience of having books delivered to your home.

PLEASE ADD $1.00 TO COVER THE COST OF POSTAGE & HANDLING.

- -

BOOKS BY MAIL

320 Steelcase Road E.,
Markham, Ontario L3R 2M1

IN THE U.S. -
210 5th Ave., 7th Floor
New York, N.Y., 10010

Please send Books By Mail catalogue to:

Name _____
(please print)

Address _____

City _____

Prov./State _____ P.C./Zip _____

(BBM1)